BUILDING

The Gilbert Girls, Book One
by Cat Cahill

---

1. http://www.catcahill.com/

Chapter One

Louisville, Kentucky - 1875

Emma Daniels was not superstitious.

She was stubborn—and a little terrified—but never superstitious. If she had been, she might have seen the weather as a sign and abandoned the railway ticket and letter of introduction in her reticule at the nearest fireplace.

As fat drops of rain splashed down on her hunter-green hat and spotted her matching skirts, she wondered if she might be better served if she *were* superstitious. After all, there had to be some comfort in believing things would go well or not simply because it rained or one saw a black cat or found a penny.

Emma clutched her reticule to her chest to protect the folded paper and ticket inside and walked as fast as decorum dictated was proper. Independence waited for her with those two items, and by some great miracle, they would also save her family.

The rain fell faster. In less than a block, her hat had drooped forward and her skirts had grown heavy. They were her nicest pieces of clothing despite being a couple of years out of date and despite the worn edges hidden under the slightly higher hem Emma had put in three days ago. Thunder rolled overhead as she passed the last of the shops. She shivered. Perhaps she could occupy her mind by composing a poem in her head about the chill of rain.

Warm to cold, the rain it weeps
From the heavens—

A frustrated sigh escaped her lips. The rain made even her poetry terrible.

The walk from the flower shop had been long enough that she should have taken a carriage—if they'd still had a driver. The drizzle had started a couple of blocks earlier, but she'd been certain she had enough time to reach the grand home she shared with her mother and three siblings before it turned into a downpour. The thought made Emma laugh aloud. At least no one else was on the street to see her acting as if she were touched in the head.

Normally, Emma took her family's current situation in stride, facing down changes she never could have imagined just a few years ago. But right now, she wished with her whole heart for a driver. She shivered again as she climbed steps flanked by late spring flowers. They'd been planted years ago when the family had the money for such things. It was as if the flowers didn't know better than to continue returning year after year.

"Ems, where have you been?" Her younger sister Lily bustled in from the parlor, face flushed from the roaring fire, to greet Emma at the door. She looked Emma up and down. "You're absolutely soaked. Come warm up."

Emma removed her hat and set it on the small table near the door, peeled off her gloves, and hung her soaked jacket, all things that Mrs. Henderson would have done had Mrs. Henderson still been with them. Their kind, trusted housekeeper had been the last servant to leave, staying for a few months even after Emma's mother had told her they no longer had funds with which to pay her.

Emma grabbed her small bag from the table and took Lily's hand. Lily was her dearest friend, but Emma hadn't even confided in her. Instead, she'd kept her trip down to the little office over the flower shop to herself. There was no need to burden her sister if the outing had been fruitless.

"Emma! We expected you home an hour ago. I had started to worry." Mama sat in the worn, large wing chair nearest the fire, her needlepoint abandoned in her lap the moment she saw her eldest daughter. "Come, sit. Tell us where you have been."

Now was the moment of truth. Emma sank gratefully into the chair opposite Mama. Her skirts felt twice their normal weight, thanks to the rain. And she'd started to shiver again.

Her youngest sister, Grace, appeared with a shawl that had seen much better days and wrapped it around Emma's shoulders. Emma smiled gratefully at her.

"I went downtown, as I said." She glanced at each member of her family. Mama, Lily, Grace, and little Joseph—who wasn't so little anymore. He grinned at her in return, and her heart melted. How could she leave them all?

"To the flower shop?" Mama's forehead crinkled. "If I'd known you'd be gone so long, I would've come with you. I'm afraid people will think it's unseemly for you to traipse about town alone."

As they always did, words such as that tugged at a little ribbon of annoyance that looped inside Emma. Was there nowhere in this world she could be alone without anyone thinking her ill-bred? "I . . . didn't go to the flower shop. Not exactly, anyhow."

Mama's brow furrowed even more. She wasn't that old, maybe forty-five at the most; Emma wasn't certain exactly. But for years she had suffered from joint problems that made her appear years older. It was hard for her to walk very far, and impossible to do much beyond home. Even the short walk to church on Sunday was almost too much for her. A trip downtown would've put her in bed for days.

"Where did you go?" Fifteen-year-old Grace watched Emma with round blue eyes.

Emma drew in as much breath as she could, no small task in her tight corset, and fixed her eyes on the frayed edges of the flowered rug that covered the wooden floor. "To an office over Jewel's Florist. There is a woman there who interviews girls for placements out West."

She dared to glance up, only to find her family staring at her. Then they spoke all at once.

"Placements? Of what sort?" Mama asked.

"Out West?" Lily wanted to know.

"What does that mean?" Grace asked.

"Are you leaving us?" Joseph said.

Emma pulled the document and the train ticket from her reticule. "She interviews for placements of all sorts, but I was particularly interested in the Gilbert Company." She passed the slightly damp papers to her mother. "They build dining rooms and hotels along the rail lines for passengers. And they need women of gentle breeding to work in the dining rooms. Can you imagine? This time next week, I could be earning money to send back to you!" The excitement rolled through her. A new place, far from the ever-present eyes of Louisville society and the whispers that followed her everywhere. She was suffocating here. Out West, she wouldn't be one of "those poor Daniels girls." She'd have to rely on herself. And to think of all the new places she'd see and the fascinating people she'd meet! The very thought sent a thrill through her.

Mama stared at the documents, blinking hard.

Emma's excitement nearly collapsed into a heap of guilt. She moved to her mother, kneeling at her side. "I don't want to leave you, of course. I love you all so much, I don't know what I'll do without you. But Mama, you know something has to change."

Mama turned to look at her, the hand clutching the letter shaking just a little. "You overheard, didn't you?"

Emma pressed her lips together and nodded. Last week, Papa's lawyer had paid Mama a visit. Emma had fetched them tea and cakes from the kitchen, only to overhear about the family's increasingly dire situation while she was standing outside the parlor door. Papa's investments hadn't been doing well thanks in large part to the ongoing depression. That she already knew. But now there was little money left in his accounts to care for the family he left behind when he passed six years ago. The lawyer had made it clear they needed to sell their home and move to a much smaller apartment, and even then, he warned that the money would only last a few months. One of them needed to obtain an income, and fast. And as the eldest, Emma knew it was her responsibility.

"I knew it was up to me. You can't—and shouldn't—do any sort of work. And I'm not about to see my sisters or Joseph go to a factory. The stories out of those places are horrible. I'd seen this advertisement a month or two ago and thought it sounded exciting. It turns out that it was just what we needed." Emma held Mama's gaze, hoping she'd understand.

Mama clutched her hand. "You could marry. Mr. Eddins asked after you just last month. Certainly that's preferable to journeying hundreds of miles to some wild place to be a serving girl. What will people say?"

Emma could have laughed, but she kept her face passive. "Mr. Eddins is far too old for me, Mama. Besides, the widow Harlow's had her eye on him for months. It won't be long before she wears him down. I have no real prospects here, you know that. And especially now that we . . ." She couldn't bring herself to say they were poor, but that was the truth of the matter. Her family's gradual decline in position was well-known in society. They'd already lost invitations to most of the usual events they'd attended in the past, and with that, any decent prospects of marriage for Emma or Lily had disappeared entirely. No man wanted to take on a bride and her entire family. Besides, she had yet to meet a man who captured her heart, and she was already nineteen years of age.

"Look here." Emma pointed at the letter of introduction in her mother's hands. "This company wants girls from good families. They'll give us a place to live together, with a chaperone, and will ensure our safety. It's good, respectable work. They'll let us have Sundays off, so I can still attend services. I'll write every week, and I'll be able to send home enough money to keep you comfortable in an apartment and pay for a doctor. They gave me a contract for an entire year. Please—" She took Mama's other hand. "Let me do this for you."

Tears rolled down Mama's face. "I cannot . . ." She swiped at her eyes. "I can't let you do this. You deserve better, my Emma." Mama ran a hand down a drying lock of Emma's hair that had come undone from the simple hairstyle Lily had created for her this morning. She tucked it behind Emma's ear.

Emma covered her mother's hand with her own. She hated to leave her family. But deep down inside . . . she'd always yearned for something more. Something exciting. Adventure. And more recently, a place where she could breathe without feeling as if everyone were pitying her. And this Gilbert Company seemed to offer exactly what she'd always dreamed of—and what her family needed.

Mama leaned her forehead against Emma's. "But I know your heart, daughter. You're just like me. Or like I was at your age." She smiled just a little, even though the tears continued to fall. "So you have my blessing."

Emma's heart raced even faster than it did when she'd first stepped foot in the office above the florist's earlier. She was going. She was really, truly *going*. Not only would she pursue her adventure, but she'd also save her family.

"I don't understand." Lily's voice made Emma stand and turn. Lily stood, her arm around Grace, who in turn held Joseph to her. "*Why* are you leaving?"

"I'll explain it to you later," Mama said. She wiped the last of the tears from her eyes and straightened her back. Even that slight movement made her wince, though she tried in vain to hide it under a smile. "Now when do you go?" She consulted the train ticket in her lap.

"Tuesday at ten," Emma supplied. She stood, gripped Lily's hand, and squeezed it. Lily forced a smile, but Emma could tell she was still upset. "I'll tell you more later," she whispered.

Lily nodded, and Emma knew she had a lot of explaining to do before Lily forgave her for not confiding in her.

"So soon," Mama whispered. She cleared her throat. "Then we'll simply have to make the most of the time you have left here."

"We'll have to go for a stroll through the park," Lily said. "Oh, I wish you'd be here to see *Romeo and Juliet* at the Macauley."

Emma nodded, even though she knew Lily wouldn't be able to afford to see the play later this summer.

"The church social is on Saturday," Grace said. "We must go to that."

"Can we watch the barges on the river?" Joseph piped up.

Emma ran a hand over his head, and he ducked away. Joseph had been enamored of the ships and barges since he was small. She was certain that one day he'd find a career with them. "We will. We'll do as much as we possibly can."

"Before you run off and marry some wild cowboy out West," Lily teased, her smile back in place, although a bit uncertain at the edges.

Emma laughed. "That won't happen. Courting isn't allowed until I fulfill my contract." She kept the rest of her thoughts to herself—the ones that said she'd likely never marry now that she had a family to support.

"Now sit, all of you," Mama said. "Emma can tell us everything, starting with where she's going."

Chapter Two

Cañon City, Colorado Territory

"Where did it go?" Monroe Hartley muttered under his breath as he searched his saddlebag for the black silk tie. It was his nicest one—the one that made the best impression.

It was also his only one.

Pender, his dappled gray gelding, sniffed and shook his head.

"Be still." He looked up at the horse to make the words sink in.

Pender snuffled again, a long piece of black silk dangling from his teeth. Monroe snorted and then laughed. Laughing wasn't something he did all that often anymore, and it felt odd. Pender was more trouble than he was worth, but the truth was, Monroe had a soft spot bigger than Pike's Peak for the horse. "Give me that." He gently pulled the silk from Pender's mouth and tied it around his neck. It was hard to tell how it looked without glass to see himself in. It would just have to do. He grabbed his hat from the saddle, adjusted it over dark hair that badly needed a cut, and patted the horse before making his way up the nearby steps to the hotel.

Cañon City didn't boast much in the way of fine things, and the hotel was the nicest establishment in town. Monroe stood in the lobby and let his eyes adjust to the dimmer light. It was quiet inside, especially given that the dining area to the left was closed. Straight ahead, a young man waited at the front desk. He appraised Monroe eagerly, most likely ready to filch a new guest out of good coin.

Monroe approached him. "I'm looking for a Mr. James Gilbert, Junior."

The desk clerk's smile flickered for a moment. He opened the large book in front of him and ran his finger down the page.

"Ah, yes. Gilbert. Room 7. Upstairs and to the left." He pointed toward the staircase.

Monroe nodded his thanks and made his way up the bare staircase. It was shadowy, and he had to duck his six-foot-one frame when he had just about reached the top. He turned and assessed the staircase. It needed a rebuild on the sloping steps that led to the third floor. Badly. Monroe hadn't been in that many fine hotels, but he had a builder's eye. He always had.

And that was exactly why he was here.

Leaving the staircase behind, he made his way to room number seven, straightened the old but clean frock coat he wore, and knocked confidently on the door. After a brief moment, it opened, revealing a man just slightly older than Monroe's twenty-four years, clad in shirt and trousers with suspenders dangling from his hips.

"Good afternoon, sir. I'm Monroe Hartley. We spoke briefly last night." Monroe held out his hand.

The other man shook it as comprehension dawned across his face. He rubbed his head and then opened the door wider, inviting Monroe inside. "I apologize for my appearance. It was a late night."

Monroe nodded. It had been, but excitement had woken him up after only a few hours' sleep, when normally he welcomed the long undisturbed sleep a night of drinking gave him. Those were the nights he didn't dream of her, although he still woke up feeling the loss and its accompanying guilt anew. Mr. Gilbert gestured to a set of stiff-backed chairs placed next to a plain wooden table by the window. Monroe took one and removed his hat.

Mr. Gilbert pulled up his suspenders and found a waistcoat lying across a washbasin. He buttoned it before fishing two cigars from the pocket of another coat draped over the back of his chair. He held one out to Monroe, who held up his hand. "It was a late night," he echoed by way of explanation. Truth be told, his stomach hadn't been right since he woke up, and now was not the time to tempt fate.

Gilbert struck a match. As soon as the cigar lit he sat down and fixed his gaze on Monroe. "You're the builder, right?"

Monroe nodded. "Yes, sir. Finest builder this side of Denver." It was only a slight stretching of the truth. He was good at the trade, after all. Never mind that his experience consisted of barns and houses and the occasional mining company office.

"My father usually contracts with folks back East." Gilbert puffed on his cigar.

This, Monroe had prepared for. "I don't charge back East prices. If you work with me, not only will it be more economical, your hotel and dining establishment will be completed much sooner. In fact, I could break ground within four days."

Gilbert furrowed his considerable eyebrows. "It would take you an entire day simply to get to Denver to hire a crew."

"One day to get there, one day to hire, one day to get them to the valley, one day to start. And that's a promise."

"Hmm." Gilbert assessed him in a way that Monroe knew was in his favor. "You haven't even seen the blueprints."

"I can build anything." And *that* was not stretching the truth. He knew he could, even if his experience was not all that extensive.

Gilbert turned and pulled a long roll of paper from the small valise on the floor behind him. Cigar clamped in his mouth, he rolled the pages out onto the table. Monroe stared at them eagerly. He could read them decently well—enough to know measurements and where windows and such went—but he'd never studied the art of building, not formally. If Gilbert got detailed with his questions, he'd need to bluff his way through them somehow.

"One main building, as you can see." Gilbert pointed to the topmost page. "The hotel, with a dining establishment, and dormitories for the young ladies and other employees who come to work for the company, all attached. Then assorted outbuildings." He flipped through the pages and glanced up at Monroe. "How long do you think this would take you?"

Monroe did some quick mental calculations. If the crew was large enough and he didn't run into any trouble . . . It would have to be done at a breakneck speed. In fact, it was almost impossible, but he needed a way in—something that would make him more desirable than any firm back East—and this was it. "Two and a half months for the hotel, provided the materials are readily available. Including the outbuildings, three months." He knew that was much faster than what any established building company would have quoted Gilbert. It would be hard work to get it built that quickly, but he also knew the only way he would get this job would be to be faster and cheaper than anyone else.

If Gilbert was surprised by the timeline, he didn't show it. "Cost? Considering the company purchases all materials, of course."

With a large crew working fourteen hours a day for ten to eleven weeks, and then another few weeks for outbuildings . . . He added it up as best he could and tossed out a number he knew would be lower than anyone else could possibly offer.

"You could get it done for that? All of it?" Gilbert rolled up the blueprints.

"Yes, sir."

"What else have you built?"

Monroe drummed his fingers on the bottom of the chair. This was one he'd rehearsed in the wee hours of the morning when he couldn't sleep. There was no way to hide the fact he'd never headed up a project of this magnitude before. He'd simply have to hope that Gilbert was still willing to take a chance on him. "A number of homes in Denver, the offices of the Tula Mining Company, an office building for the Mountain Pacific Railroad, nearly all the outbuildings at the Double Z Ranch outside Denver, and other homes and outbuildings near the Double Z. All of my customers have been satisfied with my work."

Gilbert's large eyebrows knitted together. "Are you certain you can handle a project of this size? My father and I expect nothing less than perfection."

Monroe placed both hands on the table and leaned forward. "More than certain. And I am nothing if not driven toward excellence. You won't be disappointed—in the project or in the savings to your company—if you hire me."

"Then I think you've got yourself a job." Gilbert held out his hand, and Monroe shook it gladly. "If you can keep on schedule. In fact, if you can complete the hotel building within two and a half months, I'll personally see to it that you receive additional payment." He paused a moment. "I'm taking quite a gamble on you. Don't make me wish I hadn't."

Monroe nodded. "Thank you, sir. You won't be disappointed. I'll head on up to Denver and get a crew."

"There's one more item your men will need to understand," Gilbert said as Monroe opened the door. "The girls are to be left alone."

"Girls?" Monroe raised an eyebrow. Not that he had any complaint about whorehouses, although he had already found they were useless when it came to filling the empty space in his heart.

"Girls will be coming in to train as waitresses for the dining room. They're respectable ladies from back East. My father insists on the highest standards for his facilities. Any man ruins one of those girls, and he's gone."

"Ah. Understood." Monroe tipped his hat. "I'll see you in four days." He made his way to the stairs, itching to get started.

This job should be just what he needed. Ranch work, smaller building projects, and the odd jobs he'd taken between them had left him with too many empty moments in which to think and remember. But this building should take up all his waking hours and put him to sleep so hard he'd never see a single dream.

Perhaps once this hotel was done, he'd find peace.

Chapter Three

C rest Stone, Colorado Territory

The long grasses crunched beneath Emma's sturdy black boots. The grass was different here—not thick and bright and carpeted as the spring grass had been at home. The long brown from the winter still held tight with bushels of green poking up here and there. Tiny blue-purple irises sprung up all over. It was as if spring arrived at a slower pace in these mountains. And the sagebrush . . . Emma still stared at it in wonder. One of the other girls she had befriended on the second leg of the journey from Denver to Cañon City had told her what the clumps of bushy silver-green were.

She took everything in as she waited for the other three girls to leave the wagon that the Gilbert Company had sent to collect them, rather than waiting for the twice-weekly stagecoach to arrive. Everything was different here. The sharp, steep blue mountains, some with snow at their peaks, rose to the west of her while smaller, rounder mountains stood farther off to the east. Meanwhile, the valley all around her stretched on and on, flat and brown and muted green. Even the sky looked different. It was larger somehow, the clouds whiter and fluffier than back home. And the air! Emma drew in as deep a breath as she could. It was cool—almost cold, really—but ever so clean. She could draw a deeper breath here than she ever could at home.

It was beautiful.

"It's terrifying, is it not?" Caroline, a diminutive blonde Emma had met upon boarding the wagon, closed into Emma's side. She shivered a little, and Emma wondered if it was from cold or fear.

"It's lovely," Emma said. She tucked an arm through Caroline's. The girl was only slightly younger than Emma, but she reminded Emma of fifteen-year-old Grace at home. "You needn't fear. After time, you'll grow familiar with it."

"I haven't seen any of the miners," Caroline said.

"Mr. McFarland told me some of them were a few miles from here." Apparently silver was all the rage in this part of the Colorado Territory, and mines dotted the valley from north to south.

Caroline chewed on her lip and gazed at their surroundings, her eyes landing on the skeleton frame of what looked like a large building. Men walked to and fro, carrying beams of wood, while others knelt on the ground or stood on ladders and pounded in nails.

"Now what do you suppose that will be?" Penny asked as she joined Emma and Caroline. "And who do you suppose *they* are?"

Emma choked back a laugh as Penny scrutinized the men doing the work. Penny had been her lively companion during the three-hour train ride south from Denver. At first, Emma hadn't known quite what to make of the girl. She was a year younger than Emma, but acted years older and much worldlier. Some of the things she said were downright scandalous. Emma wondered how Penny had made it past the Gilbert Company's interview. But she was glad Penny was here. Something about the girl from North Carolina put Emma at ease.

Caroline, however, stared at Penny with wide eyes. "You shouldn't speak of men so."

Penny laughed, and some of her golden brown curls fell loose from her hat. "It's not as if they're able to hear me."

"Mr. McFarland said to make our way to that white building and ask for Mrs. Ruby." The last of their small group, Dora, pointed to the largest completed building.

Emma shaded her eyes with her hand. The brim of her once fashionable maroon hat was nowhere near wide enough to keep out the afternoon sun. From the barn where they stood, the white house sat several feet away across a trampled yard with a few outbuildings. A small collection of older buildings—one about to fall in on itself, another nothing more than a shanty—stretched southward. Railroad tracks cut through the grasses, and then up a slight hill, the new construction towered over it all.

"This is what is left of the railroad town," Mr. McFarland said in his Irish brogue as he joined them. He pointed to the old buildings just past the white house before hefting Emma's trunk onto his shoulder. "The missus and me live in that little shanty. Now, ladies, if you'll follow me."

"I wonder if it isn't too late to catch a train elsewhere," Caroline murmured as she glanced back at the wagon.

Emma squeezed her arm before letting her go. "It will be fine, you'll see." She wasn't entirely certain that the sentiments she spoke were true, but she hoped they were. Out here, in this wide open space, anything was possible. Her heart thumped as she walked with the other girls after Mr. McFarland. Whether it was with anticipation or fear, she wasn't certain.

It took but a few seconds to cross the open area between the barn and the house. The constant hammering and shouts from the workmen drew Emma's attention again as they rounded the house, and she couldn't help but marvel at what they had created so far. That men could build something out of nothing was a miracle worth a moment's reflection. "Is that to be the new hotel?" she asked Mr. McFarland.

"Yes'm. One of the largest the Gilbert Company's undertaken to date, too. Seems old Mr. Gilbert believes this new railroad line from Denver to Santa Fe will draw quite the crowd." Mr. McFarland caught the trunk as it began to slide off his shoulder.

"How many folks do you think will come down this way?" Penny asked in her slight Southern drawl.

"Mr. Gilbert said it was very popular, the idea of this new line. When he told people about it back in New York and Boston, they all got excited."

"Boston?" Caroline asked, her soft voice sounding even more fearful.

"Yes'm. Apparently all them Northerners want to take the desert air."

"Isn't that where you're from?" Penny asked Caroline.

"Yes," was all Caroline said, and Emma was sure the girl shrunk into herself even more. Perhaps home was not the happy memory for Caroline that it was for the rest of them.

Home. Longing inched its way through Emma. She wondered what her family was doing right now. Maybe Lily was starting supper, and Grace was reading aloud while Mama worked on her needlepoint and Joseph chased the cat. She longed to be with them, but at the same time, she didn't want to leave.

How was it possible to wish to be in two places at once?

It was selfish to want to stay, but she needed the money. So perhaps it wasn't selfish at all. And why not enjoy herself if she had to find a way to support her family?

Emma sighed. It was the same argument she'd had with herself all the way West. One thing was for certain—no matter her own desires, nothing was going to get in the way of her earning money for her family.

"Hartley!" Mr. McFarland called to a lean, tall figure who crossed the tracks.

Emma paused with the other girls in front of the house. When the tall man grew closer, Emma gasped, audibly enough that Caroline turned to her.

"I'm fine," Emma whispered.

But it was an untruth. In fact, her breathing came as fast as if she had run from the barn across the yard rather than walked at a leisurely pace. Her hands grew hot underneath her demure gray gloves, and suddenly she needed a glass of water. She could not pull her gaze from this man. He was nearly a foot taller than she, with hair as dark as hers, and warm brown eyes. He wore a black hat that had seen better days, and he desperately needed a shave. As he stopped in front of Mr. McFarland, he caught her staring at him. She swallowed hard and looked at the ground, uncertain what to do with her eyes in such a compromising position.

"Good afternoon, ladies," he said, and when Emma dragged her gaze back up, he stared at her boldly while removing his hat. She averted her gaze to Mr. McFarland, who frowned at the man.

Mr. Hartley's easy smile vanished. "My apologies," he said quickly.

"Can you help me with the trunks?" Mr. McFarland asked, pointing at the buckboard near the barn. "I'll bring these ladies inside and be out again shortly."

Mr. Hartley nodded. As he stepped away, Emma snuck another peek at him. Sweat soaked through the back of his dark blue shirt and dirt dusted his pants.

Penny snickered. Just as Emma turned to see what she found so funny, her old trunk slid sideways off Mr. McFarland's shoulder. With a loud thud, it hit the ground, and the lock pulled apart from the old dry leather and wood.

"Oh, no!" Emma could not keep the words inside as all her worldly possessions spilled out onto the trampled grass and dirt.

As she moved toward the mess, footsteps pounded up from behind. Mr. Hartley knelt down beside her. The man she could barely keep her eyes from began picking up the strewn pieces of clothing, books, and papers that spilled from the trunk.

Emma knelt helpless beside him as he tossed in two books and held a stack of her poetry in his hand. He glanced down at it, and her face grew uncomfortably warm. He turned and gave her a curious look before he placed the papers back into the trunk. Caroline fell to her knees on the other side of Emma to help, as Penny and Dora righted the trunk and opened it all the way.

Emma blanched as she spotted a set of her underthings lying exposed next to a snowy white nightgown. She leaned forward and reached across the ground for them—just as Mr. Hartley grabbed hold of the small pile. He glanced down at his hand, and comprehension dawned across his tanned face. Embarrassment shot through Emma like lightning, warming her from head to toe, just as Mr. Hartley broke into a grin wider than the valley itself. He held out the offending clothing with a chuckle. She snatched the bundle of white cloth from his hand. His brown eyes burned with something beyond mirth, even as his face told her he found the entire situation—and her mortification—hilarious.

That look in his eyes shot to her core and made her heart take off on its own sprint. It was as if part of her had been asleep and had finally woken up. And that smile . . . The desire to suddenly leap toward him and wrap her arms around him was so strong it almost made her forget her embarrassment.

She wadded up the underthings in her hands and fixed him with what she hoped was the meanest glare she could muster.

The result being that he laughed again even as his eyes warmed to a deeper brown.

Emma had never felt so uncomfortable yet curious about someone in her life.

"It's all put back together," Dora said, and Emma was grateful for the interruption.

She yanked her attention away from this man who made her body and her mind react in the strangest ways and shoved her underthings deep into the trunk underneath layers of petticoats and dresses.

Mr. McFarland held out a hand to help her up, and all Emma could think was that she was thankful it wasn't Mr. Hartley. She couldn't imagine the effect his hand on hers would have when just his eyes sent her into a tizzy.

"I'll be glad to fix the lady's trunk for you later," Mr. Hartley said to Mr. Mc-Farland as Emma brushed the dust from her skirt.

"That would be most appreciated," Mr. McFarland said. He turned to Emma. "I apologize for dropping it. I suppose I'm not as young as I once was."

"No apology needed," Emma said, her voice a bit wobbly. "It was but an accident."

Mr. Hartley made his way back toward the wagon. And perhaps she imagined it, but it seemed as if he avoided looking at her before he left. For some reason, Emma was disappointed.

"Come along." Mr. McFarland picked up her broken trunk again, and pushed open the door with his free hand.

Emma let the other girls follow him inside first. While she waited, she turned toward the wagon. The man called Hartley walked with purpose toward the vehicle.

Emma shivered and wrapped her arms around herself. She needed to avoid him. There was no time for the feelings that had come over her when he was near, not if she wanted to keep her position and support her family.

She would keep away from him, that was all.

Chapter Four

Slapping his hat against his thigh, Monroe watched Mr. McFarland disappear into the house with the last trunk. A smile crept across his face as he remembered the dark-haired girl's embarrassment when he accidentally picked up a set of her underthings. Was she ever beautiful. And she seemed the sort who didn't know it. Those bright green eyes, skin that looked so soft his fingers had itched to touch it, a lemon scent that made him think of far-off places, dark hair piled into a cloud under her hat. He could just see himself taking that hat off and loosening her hair, running his fingers through it, pulling her to him . . .

And under no uncertain terms would any of that ever happen. Monroe shook his head to clear any last thoughts of that dark-haired beauty from his mind and slapped his hat back in place. She was forbidden—Gilbert had made that clear enough—if he wanted to keep this job. He turned toward the structure that was rising out of nothing and smiled with satisfaction.

The work did what he'd intended it to do. He'd barely had time to think of Colette, not with rising before dawn, organizing his men for the day, and working with scarcely even a break for the noontime meal until dusk. At night, he played cards with some of the crew and fell into bed bone-tired. No dreams, and hardly any soul-crushing sadness when he awoke in the morning.

That woman . . . She snuck her way into his mind again as he crossed the open ground between the house and the building site. It was the first time he had felt anything like that since Colette. He thought he might feel guilty, as if he was betraying the one woman he had ever loved with every part of his being. The guilt didn't come—at least not for that particular reason—but that lurking sadness still ate at the fringes of his consciousness, waiting to take over as soon as his mind stilled.

Monroe refused to let it still.

Across the tracks, his foreman's voice echoed. John Turner had been invaluable, even though he offered more opinions than Monroe would have liked. He kept the men in line, and that was his job, although Monroe often wondered if he should have placed Big Jim Daley, Turner's right-hand man, in the position instead. Unlike Turner, Big Jim didn't feel the need to tell Monroe how he would have preferred to frame the building or to start later in the morning. Turner was new to this work, Monroe needed to remind himself. He'd learn. And he excelled at keeping the men at task, which was what had earned him the foreman position.

Monroe stepped over the rails and boards that would carry passengers to Arizona and stopped to look down the tracks. To the south, they continued on and on into the horizon. According to Gilbert, the rail crews were nearing Santa Fe and should be finished within the next couple of months—the deadline Monroe had promised. No wonder Gilbert had jumped at his offer. The railroad company was already booking passage for the first trip down this new line in early August, and the hotel needed to be ready by that time, furniture and all.

If Monroe didn't have the place built by the time the furniture arrived, he could stop dreaming of the bonus Gilbert had promised. The money he stood to gain upon the completion of the work was something he could have only imagined until now. It would be enough to buy a piece of land, build a small place, maybe purchase some cattle—if he had a mind to do that sort of thing. Settling down with a herd of cattle did not seem the least bit appealing to him. Not to mention all those empty, lonely hours he would need to fill somehow in order to keep the memories of Colette, and the guilt he felt for what he'd done to her, at bay.

Instead, he would likely bank his earnings as he moved on to more work. This hotel would put him right where he needed to be to gain the work he wanted. More hotels, businesses, large homes, factories . . . The possibilities were endless. It was much better that he stay on the move, building place after place.

The image of the dark-haired girl he'd met earlier appeared in his mind. Green eyes, blushing to the roots of her hair, an unharnessed smile when he looked at her. He wondered how she felt about cattle ranching. She looked like a city girl. No doubt she was from back East somewhere. But unlike the diminutive blonde who clung to her side, who appeared as if the wind would blow her into the cottonwoods down by the creek, this woman stood on the land as if she'd been born and bred here, as if she were a part of it.

Monroe let out a frustrated groan. There he went again, thinking of that dark-haired angel. He needed to forget about her, and fast. This work was what mattered. Finishing this job, and then moving on to find another now that he would have a reference. Days filled with a flurry of hammers, sawing, measuring, creating something useful.

And no time to think.

Chapter Five

An older woman with graying brown hair hidden under a white cap ushered the girls through a hallway and into a kitchen at the rear of the house. The woman wore a starched dove-gray dress with a pristine apron. She gestured at the table and chairs in the middle of the room. "Please, sit."

Emma sat at the end of the table, nearest the door that was open to catch the cool spring breeze. Dora and Caroline settled in, facing each other, on either side of Emma while Penny sat in the chair nearest the stove. The older woman sank gracefully—and almost gratefully—into a chair at the head of the table opposite Emma. The kitchen was clean and welcoming, if not a bit on the warmer side, and the woman had greeted them with a smile at the door. More than ever, Emma knew she had made the right decision by taking this position. To live in this beautiful place with these friendly girls seated around her, to fill her days with meaningful work that meant her family could live comfortably back home—it meant everything. She placed her hands in her lap and tried to look as though she deserved to be here.

"Welcome to the Crest Stone Hotel and Restaurant. Such as it is, at this point," the older woman said, resting her hands on the polished oak table that had to have come from somewhere back East. "You've met Mr. McFarland. He'll manage the hotel, and his wife will keep the books. I'm Mrs. Florence Ruby, and I am the dining manager and house mother for you girls."

Emma watched Mrs. Ruby in awe. A woman managing the dining establishment—it was unheard of. She immediately liked Mrs. Ruby, based on her smile and that fact alone.

"As you can see, our future building is underway on the other side of the tracks. It will be finished in August, when our first guests will begin arriving. More girls will come before then so we may be ready, but you are the first."

Penny caught Emma's eye and grinned. Emma smiled back, just slightly. She shared Penny's enthusiasm but wanted Mrs. Ruby to know she had Emma's full attention.

"While we wait for guests, I'll be training you in the art of serving. You'll learn the proper way to set a table, greet guests, tell them what we have available to eat, serve them their meals, collect payment, and attend to any other needs they may have. By August, you'll be capable of doing all of this in under thirty minutes for guests who need to reboard their cars, but also at a more leisurely pace for those who will stay the night with us.

"For a short while, you will also be cooking meals and keeping house here. We'll have kitchen help, busboys, and girls who will work as maids once the larger building is completed, but for now, we all have to help in every way we can. I hope this is not too much of a shock to you." Mrs. Ruby glanced at each of them in turn, with an expression that let them know she would be highly disappointed if any of them objected.

Caroline's face contorted into a grimace for the briefest of moments until she replaced it with a tiny, forced smile. Emma didn't hold it against the girl. Caroline seemed quite delicate, almost as if she had been raised in the highest echelons of society. Not for the first time since she had met Caroline, Emma wondered what brought her here and how reluctant her parents must have been to allow her to come West to work as a waitress.

"We're all happy to help out wherever we might be needed," Penny spoke for the group.

Mrs. Ruby blessed her with a wide smile. "I'm glad to hear that. You were chosen not only because of your impeccable upbringing and manners, but also because you each have a degree of fortitude and adaptability."

Dora smiled as if these were the nicest compliments anyone had ever paid her. "Thank you," she said softly.

"You're very welcome, dear," Mrs. Ruby replied. "Now, while you're an employee of the Gilbert Company, we expect you to adhere to the highest standards."

Emma leaned forward to better hear Mrs. Ruby. The sounds of hammering and the shouts of the men outside had grown louder. There was laughter and she could clearly make out one man shouting directions to the others. It was him, she knew it. The man whom Mr. McFarland had called over to help him with the trunks. He must have retrieved them all from the wagon. She wondered if he had come inside or left them by the door. And if he had come inside, had he looked around the entryway for her? Did he wonder where she had gone?

She clasped her hands tighter in her lap. This line of thinking was pointless. Whyever was she thinking about a man who had embarrassed her before she had even set foot inside the establishment where she was to work? A man who looked rougher around the edges than any man she had ever known back home, despite his position here.

And yet . . . those eyes that had warmed her to her very core and seemed to see to every corner of her soul at the same time. Hair that badly needed a cut as it fell from under his hat. The way he was poised to laugh at such an embarrassing situation rather than fumble through apologies. Hands that betrayed how hard he worked.

Dear God, let me forget about him, she prayed, even as her face grew warm again. What she would give for a fan right now! Instead, she turned her head just slightly to catch the breeze wafting in from outside. And she tried to fixate on what Mrs. Ruby was saying.

"Decorum is essential to Gilbert Company employees, as I'm certain you were told in your interviews. Your dress and apron must be clean and starched at all times. You will receive two dresses, three aprons, and a cap. Your hair and hands must be neat. You will speak in quiet, respectful, but confident tones." Mrs. Ruby went on, detailing all the expectations for the girls.

Emma paid close attention, mostly to ensure she did not accidentally violate some unknown rule, but also to keep her mind from wandering back to Mr. Hartley and the way he seemed to know exactly who she was just by looking at her. Hartley . . . she had presumed that must be his last name. Mr. McFarland hadn't seemed to feel the need for proper introductions. What was his given name, then? James? Francis? William? Herbert? Emma stifled a giggle with her hand, pretending it was a cough. It couldn't possibly be Herbert. His name needed to be like him—strong, bold, warm. A name that matched that look in his eyes. The look that made her break out in goose pimples, even while inside the house and perfectly warm.

" . . . Most important of all."

Those words snapped Emma's attention back to the conversation at hand. She barely had time to be thoroughly irritated at herself for letting her mind wander back to that Mr. Hartley again, because Mrs. Ruby held each of their gazes, one at a time. Emma cleared her throat just slightly as Mrs. Ruby's watery blue eyes landed on her own. She forced herself to sit up straight and hold Mrs. Ruby's gaze. She prayed she projected a woman who was raised gently but with great strength. The perfect fit for the Gilbert Company.

"You are all ladies of good character, so I recognize that this most likely will not be an issue. But still, I must instruct you about it." Mrs. Ruby folded her hands together and leaned forward. "The Gilbert Company prides itself on operating beacons of civilization in places that can be rather . . . lawless. I trust you all remember the interviews you underwent before you were hired?"

Emma nodded with the rest of the girls. To her right, Dora shifted a little in her seat. She was likely hungry. Emma certainly was. It had to be past six o'clock, and the last meal she had eaten was breakfast on the train from Denver this morning.

"Mr. Gilbert will tolerate nothing that proves to be scandalous. He wants his establishments to be of the highest class. That means anything unseemly will result in your immediate dismissal. I doubt I need to name these, but these offenses would include thievery of any sort, insolence to your superiors, a poor attitude toward guests, not abiding by curfew, any fraternization with men—be they guests or employees or otherwise, or any other behaviors that might tarnish the Gilbert name while you are under your contract here. Any courting must wait until you have served out your contract. Do you all understand and agree?"

"Yes, ma'am," Emma said in echo of the other girls, even as her mouth went dry. She had already put her work here in jeopardy before she had even started. There could be no more musings about Mr. Hartley's first name, much less speaking to him again. Her family was far too important to risk.

"Good." Mrs. Ruby stood. "Let me show you to your room. While you'll only have two girls to a room when we move to the hotel, in this house you'll all need to share a room. You may take some time to freshen up and unpack before we begin preparing the evening meal."

Emma followed at the tail of the group. This was the start of her new life. A life of independence and excitement, where she could meet people of importance from all over the country, marvel at the beauty surrounding her, and support her family.

All she needed was to keep her wits about her.

Chapter Six

The girl's trunk was easy to fix. Truth be told, Monroe could have finished it an hour ago. But he was not in the mood to go with his crew to the mining encampment at the base of the mountains to drink and play cards. Being occupied was easier than saying no. And he couldn't go back to his tent until he was bone weary. Otherwise he would lie there as images of Colette appeared, one after the other, layering that ache with the guilt over actions he'd never forgive himself for.

So instead, he had spent the past three hours on a job that should have only lasted one. He had fixed the lock quickly enough, but upon inspecting the rest of the trunk, decided the straps that held the lid to the main body needed replacing. The leather had rotted away and torn in places, leaving the lid at risk of falling off even when locked. He'd wondered why the otherwise wealthy-looking girl had such an old trunk before pushing the thought from his mind to focus on the task at hand. Leather was not the sort of thing he simply had lying around, so he opted to sacrifice one of his saddlebags. He could purchase a new one in Denver once he had finished this job.

He had just finished attaching the second strip of leather cut from the saddlebag. Now was the moment of truth. Monroe took a deep breath and tested the lid, opening it, closing it, once, twice, three times. It worked perfectly. He could almost imagine the dark-haired girl's face when she saw it. He surmised that the trunk had most likely passed down through her family for years. Perhaps she clung to it for nostalgic purposes.

He shook his head. He wasn't supposed to be doing this to see her happy. He'd fixed the trunk as a favor to McFarland. And as an excuse to occupy his mind for a few hours. She had nothing to do with it.

Monroe took his time putting away the remaining leather pieces and cleaning up the scraps of wood that remained from his work on the lock. When he could do no more, he picked up the trunk and left the work area next to the new building.

Then he stopped still.

He had not thought this through at all. It had been easy enough earlier to catch McFarland outside and ask him to bring the trunk out. But now . . . McFarland was likely back in his shanty with his wife. Monroe could knock on the door of the big house, of course.

Perhaps the dark-haired girl would answer.

Deep down inside, he wanted to see her again, badly. But that would be the worst thing that could happen.

He sighed, the trunk in his arms as he stood there by the tracks, the clear sky filled with stars. The breeze picked up some, and he had shed his coat and hat when he began working. The chill air biting through his shirtsleeves and numbing his nose was enough to get him moving again. It took but a minute for him to reach the door to the house. He shifted the trunk to the left, braced it between himself and the doorframe, and knocked on the white-painted door with his right hand. Just as he heard footsteps, he spit on his hand and raked it through his hair.

The older woman that ran the place, Mrs. Ruby, opened the door. Monroe's heart sank a bit. He was being foolish. It was just as well that Mrs. Ruby greeted him.

"May I—" she began, but a shout from somewhere in the rear of the house interrupted her greeting.

"Go attend to your girls." McFarland appeared from the kitchen, wiping his face with a soft white napkin.

Mrs. Ruby disappeared from view, and McFarland turned to Monroe. "The missus and I decided to take our meal here—give these girls someone to practice their cooking on." He made a face that indicated their skills were not all he had hoped for. "It's a darned good thing they got hired on as waitresses and not cooks. I see you got that trunk all fixed up." He looked over his shoulder. "I'd let you take it upstairs yourself, but Mrs. Ruby would have my hide."

Monroe chuckled as he handed the trunk to McFarland. "I understand."

"That would've taken me at least a few days to get to. How'd you finish it so fast?"

"I was glad to have the work. Gave me something to do." Monroe ran a hand over the new leather. He wished he could see the girl's face when she saw what he'd done.

"Man who likes to stay busy." McFarland hefted the trunk onto his shoulder, and the look he gave Monroe made Monroe think he understood entirely why a man might like to keep his mind occupied. "I'll be certain to let her know who fixed it." He winked at Monroe.

"No need," Monroe said, although he felt quite the opposite. He said goodnight and walked back toward the tracks. But instead of crossing them, he headed south along the line. A good walk would thoroughly tire him out, and he would be asleep in no time at all.

He walked about a mile south, until all he could see of the house and barn and his crew's tents were pinpricks of light coming from lanterns and lamps. Along the way he plotted the next day's work. If they moved fast enough, they could complete the framing by midday. That would put them right on track to finish in the allotted time. Back in his tent, he had an exact plan laid out, week by week, for the entire project.

As he approached the house on the way back, he spotted a figure moving across the yard between the house and the outbuildings that sat out back. He squinted through the night, trying to decipher who it might be. Without thinking, he veered toward the side of the house. The figure reached the house and leaned against the wall—doing what, he had no idea. But curiosity had gotten the better of him now. It was too much to hope for that it would be her. In fact, it *shouldn't* be her, if he knew what was good for him—and her. Likely, it was Mrs. Ruby, ready to tell him exactly what she thought about him skulking around her house.

Yet, he kept walking toward the person. It was a woman, that much he could tell now. Her skirts moved in the chill night breeze, and she clutched her arms to her chest. As he moved closer, the muted light from the kitchen window illuminated her dark hair. His heart sped up. Could it be?

He should go. He knew that. But would it hurt to simply say hello? Perhaps apologize for his poor manners earlier? Ask her if she liked her trunk?

No. It was wrong. It could get him run out before the sun came up tomorrow. And it might give her the wrong idea about him. He'd promised himself that he would never subject another woman to what he'd expected of Colette.

He stopped still, decided to turn around and say not a word. He had taken one step away from the house when a voice stopped him.

"Who's there?"

He stopped again and closed his eyes. He'd acted stupidly. If only he'd listened to the intelligent part of his brain before he'd gotten this close. He turned around slowly.

The mere sight of her drew a smile to his lips.

She was gorgeous. There was no other word for it. The soft light made her look almost angelic. She wore a much plainer dress than she had arrived in. It matched Mrs. Ruby's—a light gray with what used to be a crisp white apron but now sported various food stains from top to bottom. Her hair fought to escape the white cap she'd perched on it. She watched him carefully, tucking a flyaway lock behind her ear.

"Monroe Hartley," he said by way of introduction. "We met earlier, when your trunk took a tumble."

"Oh. Yes. I remember."

The light was too shadowy to tell, but he was almost certain her face had turned that same shade of pink he had seen earlier. It was endearing, and smacked of innocence.

"I'm sorry. I shouldn't be here." He shoved his hands into his pockets.

"No, you shouldn't." She rubbed her hands up and down her arms and glanced over her shoulder. She lowered her voice when she spoke again. "But I'm glad, because I wanted to thank you for fixing my trunk. It looks almost new. You truly have a talent."

Her flattery threw him speechless.

"So . . . thank you. I must go inside now." She turned, and on a whim, he reached out and grabbed her arm. And then immediately berated himself for his impropriety. This was not the kind of woman he could do things like that with.

But she didn't pull away—not immediately. Instead, she stopped and glanced down at his hand.

He let go of her, gently and slowly. "I'd like to know your name." He hated himself for asking, but he needed to know.

She looked up at him. He would never forget the vivid green of her eyes this afternoon, though they looked much darker under the stars. Now they were fixated on him.

"After all, I've seen your underthings. The least I should know is your name." He shot her his best smile.

"I . . ." She ducked her head, and he just knew her face held that pretty blush again.

He watched her breathe as she contemplated his request. He could barely breathe himself, wondering if she was going to send him away, nameless.

Finally she looked up, and a small smile played on her face. "You may call me Miss Daniels." A clatter sounded from within the house. With a start, she retreated inside, leaving him standing alone in a place he should—without any question—never have been.

Miss Daniels. It made him laugh out loud as he crossed the tracks back toward the tents. It was a challenge, and Monroe Hartley never passed on a challenge, even when every fiber of his being warned him against it.

"Evening, Boss." John Turner fell into step next to him. "What's the plan tomorrow?"

Monroe pushed thoughts of Miss Daniels from his mind. Work was what he should be focusing on. "Finish the framing by noon. Then we move on to siding." A train had arrived a few days ago with everything they needed for the walls before it returned north to Cañon City.

Turner paused. "It would be best to put the lath on first. Start with the interior walls rather than the exterior."

Monroe scowled at the ground. "Siding first to give the lath some protection from the elements."

"All right then, Boss."

Turner continued to walk alongside him. It would be one thing if the man simply offered a decent suggestion here and there, but Turner was more inclined to state an unfounded opinion, or worse, question Monroe's every decision. He gritted his teeth and reminded himself to be patient. After all, no one was born knowing all there was to know about building. He'd been just as ignorant a few years ago. The one thing Turner didn't have to learn was how to keep the crew working. And that was important, Monroe reminded himself often.

When they reached Monroe's tent, Turner made no move to go to his own tent.

"Something else you need?" Monroe asked.

Turner shook his head. His jaw worked, almost like he was itching to say something.

Monroe waited, not entirely patient.

"I just wanted to say thank you." Turner rubbed a hand over his shaved chin. "For taking me on as foreman. I know I get ahead of myself sometimes." He glanced off to his left, where the hotel stood in darkness. "I want to head up my own crew one day. Be in charge of building grand places like this one."

Monroe relaxed, air rushing through his teeth. He'd suspected Turner was simply ambitious, and confirming it warmed a corner of his heart. The man was more like him than he'd wanted to see. "This is as good a place as any to learn, I suppose. And you're halfway there, seeing how you keep the men on schedule. Get some sleep. You've got some walls to build tomorrow."

Turner grinned, almost like an eager little boy. He thanked Monroe and then disappeared toward his tent.

When Monroe lay down, thoughts of Turner and the hotel and his schedule slid away. But the emptiness didn't hit him until just before he fell asleep.

Miss Daniels certainly did a good job of keeping his mind occupied.

Chapter Seven

Every part of Emma ached. Her feet, her legs, her sides, her arms, even her neck. The work was much harder than she had bargained for, but she refused to give in. Reaching into the basket of clean linens, she pulled out yet another wet bedsheet and flung it over the line that crisscrossed its way between several wooden stakes hammered into the ground.

Caroline leaned against one of the poles, her eyes closed.

"Are you feeling well?" Emma asked.

Caroline nodded, her eyes still closed. "I think so."

"You mustn't give in to it. That feeling of wanting to crawl up the stairs and throw yourself into bed," Emma clarified.

Caroline opened her eyes. She smiled softly at Emma. "I know. I'm trying. It's simply that this is so much . . . more than I ever thought it might be."

"It will get easier." Emma pulled a clothespin from the pocket of her apron—one of the three she had treated with baking soda nearly every night to remove the stains from all of her cooking and serving mishaps.

"When the maids and the kitchen staff come, I know." Caroline pushed herself away from the pole and reached into the basket for a towel.

"Hang the bedsheets," Emma said as she clasped the last clothespin onto her sheet. "I'll hang those. They're heaviest."

Caroline chewed on her lip. Then she took the towel anyway.

Emma hid a smile by looking in the other direction. As shrinking as Caroline might seem at times, she had a will of steel. All of the girls had tried—Penny more than once—to get her story out of her, but all Caroline would say was that circumstances beyond her control had forced her to leave her well-to-do family in Boston. Though come to think of it, none of them had been particularly forthcoming with why they were here. All Emma had told her new friends was that she needed to support her family. She'd left out the more dire details.

After the evening meal, Emma offered to retrieve the dry laundry while the other girls set about cleaning the kitchen and preparing the items needed for the next morning's breakfast. Basket under her arm, she made her way outdoors. She paused on the little stoop just outside the door and drew in a breath of the clean, cool air. *This* was why she asked for the chore of taking down, ironing, and folding all the linens and towels—for a few stolen moments of chill breeze on her skin, the distant Wet Mountains dancing in her vision, and the glory of the setting sun behind her over the massive Sangre de Cristos. It was nearing midsummer, and with it came a strong desire to be outside, soaking in every last ray of sunshine.

Emma nearly laughed to herself as she stepped lightly down the stairs to the ground. She'd begun to develop a few freckles across her nose, thanks to the small cap she wore here instead of the usual wider-brimmed hat she would've worn at home. Mother would be appalled. But here . . . it didn't seem to matter. The only person she hoped to impress was Mrs. Ruby, and all Mrs. Ruby cared for was work done well and good manners.

As she unpinned a sheet from the line, Emma reveled in the colors the sun created as it headed toward the horizon behind her. While the tall mountains obscured its final descent, the oranges and purples and pinks it brought forth shot above the peaks into the sky, making the entire valley look like some sort of wonderland. How lucky she was to live here. When she interviewed for the position, the woman at the office claimed Emma could be sent any number of places—the desert of Arizona, the plains of Kansas, the shores of California. But somehow, by some blessed intervention, she had landed here in this magnificent place. She only wished she could share its beauty with her sisters. How they would love it! Lily would chatter on nonstop about the views while Grace would sit quietly and attempt to replicate the sunset in paints. Emma smiled thinking about it. She had tried to put the majesty of the landscape into more than one poem, but had yet to write one that did it justice.

Voices from behind the barn drew her attention away from her own thoughts. Mr. McFarland appeared, hands in his pockets. He nodded to Emma and made his way through the yard, toward his own shanty. Just as he rounded the corner of the house, the breeze stirred into a wind, picking up the small cloth in Emma's hand and sending it sailing across the yard toward the barn.

Emma moved to retrieve it, but the wind only caught it again. She picked up her skirts and began to run after it. It was not particularly ladylike, but the last thing she wanted to do was explain to Mrs. Ruby that the wind had stolen a cloth from her. The inevitable stains from the dirt would be enough to fret about. She passed the barn and finally snatched the cloth from the ground—only to find herself face-to-face with Monroe Hartley.

"Good evening, Miss Daniels." He took off his hat. "Runaway laundry?"

Emma stood up straight, smoothed her skirts, and tried to catch her breath. How was it this man found her at, yet again, a most inopportune time? She held up the cloth. "As you can see, I've caught it." Her voice came out a bit breathy. She waited for her body to relax, but it did no such thing.

"It was an excellent display of athleticism." A smile tugged at the corners of his lips.

Emma clasped her hands together in front of her, the cloth imprisoned between them. Her heart hammered, and she glanced down at Mr. Hartley's work to keep from catching his eye.

His gaze followed hers to the length of wood lying on a bench next to him. It had hinges on its side, and for the life of her, Emma could not place it.

"Stall door," Mr. Hartley supplied. "The latch came off. I'm attempting to repair it."

"Isn't that Mr. McFarland's work? Until the stable hands arrive, I mean."

Mr. Hartley shrugged. "It is. I offered to do it so he could attend to other business."

Emma looked up at him. For a moment, his face looked almost vacant, as if he was somewhere else. "You do like to keep busy," she finally said.

The warm smile was back. "I do. And what do you do to keep busy, *Miss Daniels*?" The emphasis on her name drew a smile to her own lips. "Oh, wait, I remember! You write poetry."

Her face went warm. His words brought that embarrassing moment back to mind—the contents of her trunk strewn across the ground, baring her entire life to a man she hadn't even been properly introduced to.

"I do," she said carefully. "It isn't very good."

"I'd like to hear some." His eyes held hers, and she swallowed hard. The teasing smile was absent now. Was he serious? Why would he want to hear her amateur attempts at rhyme?

"I . . ." Words had entirely disappeared from her vocabulary. As she searched for something to say, a whistling sounded from behind her. Emma started. With a last quick glance at Mr. Hartley, she moved with purpose back toward her basket of laundry. "The wind took my cloth," she said by way of explanation when she drew closer to Mr. McFarland.

"Aye," he said, a tool of some sort dangling from his hand. "It's strong tonight. You'd best get inside. I fear a storm is a-brewing."

Emma nodded. He moved on, and she swallowed her fear of being found alone with Mr. Hartley. She tossed the cloth into the basket and plucked another sheet from the line. In just a few days, she would be able to post an envelope with money back to her family in Kentucky. She couldn't risk losing that.

The best thing to do would be to not speak to Mr. Hartley again. There was nothing impolite about simply nodding to acknowledge his presence and then moving on about her business. As she opened the back door to the house, basket under her arm, that was exactly what she resolved to do, despite the curiosity that nagged at her heart.

"I THINK HE'S QUITE handsome." Penny cupped her chin in her hand, the napkin in front of her completely forgotten.

"Well, *I* think we'd all be wise to keep to ourselves." Caroline creased the pristine white linen into perfect folds, just the way Mrs. Ruby had shown them earlier. "If we wish to stay here, of course."

"I didn't say I'd do anything about it. I'm simply making an observation you'd have to be blind not to see," Penny replied. She plucked her napkin up between two fingers, sighed, and dropped it back to the table. "I will never get this right."

"Here." Caroline reached for the piece of cloth and slowly showed Penny the correct folds again.

Emma kept her eyes fixed on Caroline's work, happy to see how Caroline had gained some confidence today. She'd done well with all the tasks Mrs. Ruby had set before them that morning, and the praise had seemed to do wonders for her.

"Don't you girls agree with me?" Penny asked.

Dora made an unladylike shrug. "He's awfully fair."

"Like a man from Norse legend," Penny said defensively. "Emma? Don't you agree with me?"

"I suppose," Emma said, keeping her voice as neutral as possible. Penny may have been talking about another man on the building crew, but the only face Emma saw in her own mind was that of Mr. Hartley. The thought warmed her to her toes, and she didn't dare meet any of the other girls' eyes.

She could almost hear the smile that crossed Penny's face. "Our Emma doesn't think my Norse god holds a candle to the gentleman who fixed her trunk."

Emma's face burned. "I said no such thing."

"You don't need to. Your face says it all." Penny lifted her chin in victory.

"Oh, hush," Caroline said, making the last crease in Penny's napkin. "Emma has more important things on her mind. Such as learning this technique." She held the finished napkin up.

"All I want is to keep my position here," Emma said.

"We *all* want that," Penny replied. "But what's the harm in simply looking?"

Caroline shook her head and reached for another pressed napkin from the small stack in the middle of the table.

"None," Penny answered herself. "No harm at all. Besides, would it be so terrible if one of those handsome men waltzed right up to you, proposed marriage, and took you away from all of this . . . napkin folding? Perhaps took you to San Francisco or back East? I, for one, would prefer to stay here, but you can't deny you'd rather return to civilization, Caroline."

Caroline chewed her lip, all of the confidence vanishing from her face. "I suppose not." But the words sounded almost hollow.

Emma wondered, not for the first time, what had brought Caroline here, but Penny's laugh shook her right out of her thoughts.

"If your Mr. Hartley found his way to that door right there, Emma, and asked for your hand, tell me you'd say no." Penny pushed a curl from her eyes and waited for Emma's response.

Emma pressed her lips together to keep from smiling. No one knew about her conversation with Mr. Hartley by the barn yesterday evening. Or how she'd shamelessly stood right there and let him tease her. Or how much she'd thought of him since then. It was all only a foolish distraction. One she would remain clear of in the future, she'd already determined. "I barely know the man. And I need this position."

"That's not an answer." Penny's smile widened.

"A man is hardly the answer to everything," Dora said quietly.

Penny raised her eyebrows, and Emma could see the questions forming on her face. Dora kept her eyes fixed on the napkin in front of her. As Penny opened her mouth, Emma quickly spoke instead.

"Perhaps Caroline can show us all again how she's gotten this fold so easily."

Caroline nodded, seeming to understand exactly what Emma wanted—to draw attention away from a subject that Dora seemed to want to avoid. And a subject Emma would prefer to avoid herself, given the sheer joy and fluttering nerves that flew through her entire body every time she even thought of Mr. Hartley.

As Caroline demonstrated and Penny sighed in boredom, Emma fought to keep her attention where it needed to be. Yet her thoughts kept wandering to the man with the dark hair and mischievous smile whose sole purpose in life seemed to be embarrassing her.

How could she want so desperately to see someone, yet at the same time pray for such a thing to never happen again?

Chapter Eight

All the next day, Monroe found his attention wandering from placing siding to the white house across the railroad tracks. Each time, he grew more frustrated with himself for the distraction. Near the end of the day, he was almost thankful for the crew that had moved around the rear of the hotel. He joined them, pounding nails and trying to drive thoughts of Miss Daniels from his mind.

As the sun sank behind the mountains, Monroe gestured to Turner to call the day. After the crew collected the supplies inside the large, hastily constructed shed that served to protect them from rain, some moved toward the encampment while others climbed onto horses or went on foot to the mining enclave for a night's entertainment.

"I asked Ramirez and his men to begin work on the lath in the morning." Turner appeared like a ghost.

Monroe forced himself to take a deep breath before he spoke. The man had confessed he got ahead of himself sometimes, but he was learning. Just as Monroe was about to remind him that they needed to finish the siding first, movement from behind Turner caught his eye.

It was a woman, a basket hanging over her arm, making her way along the wagon tracks that ran between the hotel and the crew's tent encampment toward Silver Creek. Dark hair, soft gray dress and white apron, and a stride that looked as if she walked on the clouds.

"Boss?"

What did it matter if a small group of men started the lath tomorrow? They were nearly finished with the siding. The rest of the men would need to begin either the lath or the floors tomorrow anyhow. Monroe yanked his eyes from Miss Daniels. "That's fine, Turner."

Turner blinked at him before allowing his face to spread into a smile of victory. "You headed over to the mining camp, Boss?"

"Not tonight," Monroe said, busying himself with angling a wheelbarrow just so against the shed wall. It was better than gluing his eyes to the woman nearing the trees that lined the creek.

"You ought to. Does a man good to spend time in the company of women and drink."

Drinking and whores and losing his shirt in a card game were useless when it came to quieting his mind. Somehow, he felt even worse after the dreamless sleep whiskey brought on. But he appreciated the thought. He clapped Turner on the back. "Maybe another night."

Turner nodded and made his way to the corral where the men lucky enough to own horses kept them.

Monroe inspected the interior of the shed and, satisfied, began his own trek toward the tents. But as he crossed the wagon tracks, he found himself looking down them toward the creek.

Silver Creek was only visible through the opening created by the wagon tracks. Cottonwoods and aspens, trees happy to find a source of water in the otherwise dry valley, obscured most of the creek. Monroe stopped, then shook his head with how strong the pull was to stride down the hardened dirt ground to catch a glimpse of Miss Daniels.

Restraint, Hartley. He needed to find some. As much fun as his banter with Miss Daniels had been, and as attracted to her as he was, it could—and it would—go nowhere. Not if either of them wanted to keep their places here. It was selfish of him to have any thoughts otherwise, after what had happened to Colette.

With every bit of determination he could muster, Monroe dragged his eyes from the trees and forced himself to move forward to the camp.

Chapter Nine

The water rushed fast and cold around Emma's hand. She withdrew it from the creek and stood up straight. Excursions to the creek to retrieve water or items from the springhouse were truly one of Emma's greatest joys in this place. She closed her eyes and breathed in the fresh air, concentrating on the beauty around her and not on the man she'd spotted behind the partially built hotel as she'd made her way down the wagon trail to the creek.

The air smelled of pine and wet sand and some sweet floral she couldn't identify. Birds sang to each other in the trees above. One day, she'd learn their names, the way she'd learned to recognize the birds' songs at home. Part of her was tempted to set aside her work for the evening and remain by the creek, composing poems, until it was too dark to see.

The air whispers, hums across my skin—

A rustling sound from behind nearly made her drop the basket she carried. She whirled around and scanned the line of trees through the stand of aspen where she stood. A split second later, a man emerged from between the trunks and leaves.

He walked slowly, straight toward her. He was young, about her age or perhaps even younger, with a crop of thick chestnut hair, a tanned face, and an easy smile. "Good evening, miss."

Emma swallowed. Her tongue suddenly felt three sizes too large for her mouth. She clutched the handle of the basket so hard, the woven wood fibers dug into her palm. Something about this felt *wrong*.

"Good evening," she forced herself to say. Perhaps all he wanted was a drink of the cool water. That was much more likely than the other scenarios racing through her mind right now.

But he stopped just short of the creek. And right next to her.

"Pardon me," she said, almost short of breath, as she backed away. "I need to get my butter."

He smiled again, but there was something about it that didn't reach his eyes. Instead, those roved over her, tracing her from the top of her head to the tips of her toes.

Emma held the basket in front of her, almost as if it could protect her from his gaze.

"What's your name?" he asked.

When she didn't reply, he added, "I'm Henry."

He didn't take off his hat. It was such a ridiculous thing to notice, but every gentleman she'd ever met in her life had removed his hat upon first meeting her.

Penny had offered to accompany her to the creek, but Emma turned her down in favor of the solitude. Why was she so hardheaded? Penny would have had the words to make this man scurry back into the hole from which he came.

"You're awful quiet." He didn't take another step toward her, yet somehow his presence grew even larger.

Emma drew herself up as straight as the aspen next to her. She had to do this without Penny, sick feeling in her stomach or not. "I'm no such thing. Now, if you please, allow me to finish my chore." She forced herself to look straight into his eyes. They were brown, like Mr. Hartley's, but held none of the warmth or humor of his.

The man laughed. "I like a woman with spirit. All I want is a bit of companionship. It's lonesome out here. Can't a good Christian woman take pity on a man like me?"

Every hair on Emma's body raised with the realization of why this man was here.

He took another step forward.

And she screamed.

Chapter Ten

Monroe was steps away from his tent when a scream sounded from the trees. It was small, almost too quiet to hear, but it was enough to stop him dead in his tracks. None of the men milling around the tents seemed to have even heard it. Monroe raced down the wagon ruts toward the creek. Glancing left and right, he took a moment before spotting her. She was almost hidden in a stand of aspen that overhung the small springhouse a little ways down the creek to the right.

Monroe's fists curled when his eyes also caught a glimpse of a man. He couldn't make the man out clearly, but Miss Daniels stood with her basket clasped to her chest, her head shaking a vigorous *no*.

He crossed the distance in no time at all, the scene becoming increasingly clearer. The man had placed his hands on her arms and was attempting to draw her closer.

"Please, stop." Her voice was laced with fear.

It propelled Monroe even faster. He burst through the trees and aimed his fist straight into the side of the man's jaw. The young man fell sideways into the spindly trunk of an aspen. "What is the meaning of this?" Monroe barked at him.

"I . . ." The man trailed off, red coloring his face, his eyes fixed on the ground as he rubbed his jaw. Monroe recognized him from Denver. He was young, maybe eighteen or nineteen. Henry, his name was.

"Don't you move," he ordered the kid.

"Miss Daniels, are you all right?" He tempered the anger in his voice when he spoke to her.

She still clutched the basket to her chest as if it would save her somehow. She was breathing hard and her eyes were wide. The urge to take her into his arms and promise her no one would ever hurt her again surged through him.

Of course, that was likely the last thing she wanted right now. He kept his hands clenched at his sides, ready to knock Henry sideways again if need be.

"I'm . . . fine." Her voice was nearly a whisper, choked on the edges.

It made him want to pummel the kid. But instead, he fixed him with a glare. "Pack your bag. You're leaving."

"Tonight?" Henry asked, his hand still rubbing at his jaw. "I don't have a horse."

"*Now*," Monroe growled. "You knew the rules. You can walk, for all I care." He took a step forward and grabbed the younger man by his shirt collar. "I don't tolerate men like you on my crew, rules or not." He let go and stepped back. "Go. I don't want to see you around when I get back."

Henry scrambled up and darted away toward the wagon tracks.

Monroe watched until he disappeared from sight. Then he turned back to Miss Daniels, who had finally let the basket fall to her side. "Are you certain you're all right?"

She ran a hand over her pinned-up hair. "I . . . I think so. Just frightened."

Her words ate through him. *"I'm frightened," Colette had said. "The way the men leer at me. And there are no women here at all. I don't want to leave the tent."* The memory seared his vision, as if she were standing before him again, and it took him a moment to shake it away.

Miss Daniels studied him, her green eyes bright in the orange light of the setting sun. "Truly, Mr. Hartley. I'm fine. He gave me a good scare, but I'm not hurt. Thank you for arriving at just the right time."

"I apologize for him," Monroe finally said. "If you like, I can inform Mr. McFarland about what happened and arrange an escort for you and the other girls each time you need to come to the springhouse."

"I'm sure that's not necessary," she said. "Besides, I enjoy the time alone. I love to walk, and this creek with the trees and the mountains behind us . . . it's simply magnificent. I'm sure another incident like that won't happen again. If Mrs. Ruby finds out, I fear she won't let us come down here any longer."

Monroe gazed at her in wonder. The woman was just attacked, and the thing she feared the most was losing her independence? It made no sense, and yet . . . He was intrigued, suddenly possessed by the desire to know everything about this Miss Daniels.

"It is beautiful here," he said instead of asking the nine hundred questions that had entered his mind. "I grew up mostly in Denver, so I fear I take it all for granted at times. I spent my youngest years in Kansas City. I doubt I could ever return there, as I'd almost certainly long for the way the peaks seem to touch the sky here."

She gifted him with a soft smile. "That's quite poetic, Mr. Hartley."

"Is it? Then I offer it to you to use in one of your poems." He held out his hand as if he were presenting her with jewels.

That made her laugh, and the sound coursed through his body, lighting him up from the inside out. All he wanted in that moment was to make this woman laugh, make her smile, and keep her safe from men like Henry. "Tell me, did you leave behind a city, rolling farmland, or perhaps some tropical paradise to come here?"

"I'm from Kentucky."

"Horse country. Does that make you a fine horsewoman, then?"

She laughed again, and all he wanted to do was laugh with her. "Not particularly. My family lived in the city. Louisville. And yes, I can ride, but only well enough to keep my seat and not tumble off onto my head."

"Perhaps that's something I'll get to see. You on a horse, that is, not falling on your head." As soon as those words were out of his mouth, he wished he could take them back. He was being too forward, and he knew it.

She fought a smile. "I need to collect my butter and return. The girls will be worrying after me." She opened the springhouse door, retrieved what she needed, and placed it in the basket. Then she straightened and took a tentative step forward.

He extended his arm as a sign she should go first. "I need to ensure that someone has left Crest Stone. But first, please allow me to escort you back to the house."

She tucked a loose strand of hair behind her ear. "I appreciate your concern, Mr. Hartley, but I'll manage on my own. I don't wish to place either of our positions at risk."

Monroe nodded. "If you're certain."

She took a step forward, then stopped and turned back to him. "Thank you. I don't know what would have happened if you hadn't arrived when you did."

"Don't think on it," he replied. Although to think of it himself made him want to put his fist into a tree trunk. Or better yet, Henry's face. "I assure you, most of my crew is honorable."

"I'm certain they are." She shifted her basket to her right hand and began to walk again toward the wagon tracks.

"Good evening, *Miss Daniels*," he called after her. If nothing else, he hoped she would relent and offer her given name.

But instead, she looked over her shoulder and only smiled at him before disappearing behind the trees.

That smile carried him toward the encampment and occupied his thoughts so thoroughly he almost walked right past his own tent.

He couldn't get this girl out of his mind. She was lemons and sunlight and happiness. This girl, he reminded himself, who could get him fired if he didn't stay away. This girl whose reputation he'd ruin if he persisted. This girl he had barely said more than a handful of words to. This girl he had no business speaking to at all given what he'd done to Colette.

Despite all of that, she danced in and out of his thoughts the rest of the evening. She even kept the blackness from consuming him before he fell asleep.

And he didn't even know her name.

Chapter Eleven

Raising her face to the sky, Emma clamped a hand on her straw bonnet as the buckboard wagon jerked to and fro. She wondered, yet again, how such a place as this could exist. The new grasses were more brilliant than they had seemed a week ago, the sky was perfectly clear, and birds sang in the few trees that dotted the valley. Now that it was late June, it was warmer than it had been so far. She marveled at how different this place was from home, where it would already be suffocatingly hot. This valley, the clear, glittering Silver Creek, the mountains on either side of her—it was truly magnificent. When she contemplated how she could've been shut away in a factory back home, she was more than thankful for this opportunity.

"That was a lovely service," Caroline said from where she was perched on a board nailed across the wagon. She sat next to Penny, who shrugged at the statement.

"Awfully dull, if you ask me," Penny said. "Back home, the preachers speak with more fire. What about you, Dora? How'd that compare to Chicago?"

Dora smiled, but tensed her hands in her lap. "It was similar," she said.

Emma watched the olive-skinned girl for a moment. The two of them sat together facing Penny and Caroline and the rear of the buckboard. Of her three new friends, Dora was the one about whom she knew the least. Perhaps she was shy. Emma hadn't wanted to push her, but she wished the other girl would find herself comfortable enough to share more about her life at home. By now, Emma knew everything about Caroline's stuffy existence in Boston as the child of a prominent family, and Penny's lively stories about her escapades in Wilmington and how they'd bothered her mother to no end—although none of them had discussed what had brought them to Crest Stone.

"I think we should stay a spell by the creek," Penny said, her hand clamped onto her hat to keep it from flying off each time the wagon bounced—which was quite often.

"We brought nothing to eat," Caroline said. "And Mrs. Ruby is expecting us."

"It's our day off, isn't it? Once the trains begin coming through, we may not get the same days off. We should take advantage of this opportunity while we have it." Penny's eyes were alight with mischief, a look Emma had gotten to know well ever since Penny had suggested they each try the cooking brandy their first week at the house. "And if you ask me, it's a welcome relief not having someone looking over my shoulder every second."

"Penny!" Caroline scolded. "Mrs. Ruby only wants to see us succeed."

"And train the new girls coming in a couple of weeks," Penny parroted. "Yes, we all know. But isn't it nice to feel *free* for a few hours?"

"I think it's a wonderful idea," Dora said.

Penny shot her a winning grin. "I knew you were one for adventure, Dora."

"Fine by me to stop for a while," Mr. McFarland said from up front where he was driving the team, his wife perched beside him. "Just so happens, Mrs. McFarland thought to bring a hunk of cheese and some bread. Figured you girls might want to make good use of the time on your own."

"You're a dear old man, Mr. McFarland," Penny teased.

"Old, huh?" Mr. McFarland pursed his lips.

"It's true, dear," his wife said with a grin. "Although I love you just the same." She gave him a peck on the cheek. During the service, Emma happened to catch Mrs. McFarland, in her blue poplin dress and matching bonnet, reach for her husband's hand. The way he had looked down on her, eyes shining with adoration, made Emma go warm with longing. It brought to mind the way her own parents had been prior to her father's death. She'd had a hard time focusing on the rest of the service, her thoughts interspersed with memories of her parents together and how hard it had been for her mother to lose her father, and flashes of Monroe Hartley and the way she had caught him watching her with something like wonder in his eyes.

She sighed. Wishing and dreaming would do her no good when there was no prospect of such a thing for her future.

"Emma?" Penny prodded.

She turned her attention back to her friends. Emma didn't see the harm in spending an extra hour or so by the creek. In fact, it sounded downright delightful. But just as she opened her mouth to say as much, a terrible cracking noise sounded from somewhere behind her, near the front of the wagon.

Dora screeched, and Emma clung to the bench as the entire buckboard tilted backward. Caroline and Penny lurched forward, crashing into Emma and Dora. Mrs. McFarland's scream sounded from up front. Emma fought to stay in the wagon as Dora's weight pushed her sideways, precariously close to the edge. The buckboard stopped in its tracks.

The horses shrieked and whinnied. "Whoa! Calm down there, boys!" Mr. McFarland called to them.

"Girls, are you hurt?" Mrs. McFarland called from right behind Emma, her voice shaking.

"No," Penny finally spoke up, breathing heavily. She pushed herself away from Caroline and onto the tilted board where she'd been sitting. She reached for Dora and helped pull her off Emma before glancing at each of the girls "I believe we're all still in one piece."

Emma nodded in agreement. Her hands shook from fear, but she wasn't hurt.

Mr. McFarland leaped from the driver's seat and came around to the side that leaned precariously close to the ground. One by one, he helped them down. Once they were all safely on firm ground, he grabbed onto the side of the wagon and lowered himself slowly to get a better look at the wheel.

Emma peered around him. The once round wheel had splintered apart near the top. The half that attached to the axle that ran under the wagon bowed out toward them under the weight.

Mr. McFarland pushed himself up with a grunt.

"Does it look like much trouble to fix?" his wife asked.

"Can't be done here. I need the smithy." He pulled off a pristine gray hat Emma had never seen him wear before today. In fact, the man wore an entire suit she would have never expected him to even own. Although he was to be the hotel manager, so perhaps he had an entire wardrobe of fine clothing hidden away for the occasion.

Mr. McFarland returned his hat to his head and reached under the buck-board's seat for a small toolbox. "I can take it off, but I'll have to bring it back to Crest Stone for Benton to fix proper. Shouldn't be more than a few hours."

"We'll wait here," Mrs. McFarland said. "The girls wanted some time alone, and so we'll have a picnic by the banks of the creek." She turned to Emma and the others. "How does that sound?"

"Like heaven," Penny said immediately.

Emma laughed, and even Caroline and Dora joined in.

"It's decided, then." Mrs. McFarland took her husband's hand and squeezed it.

He nodded and unhitched one horse from the wagon, saddled it with the saddle that had ridden in the rear of the buckboard, and lashed the wheel to the saddle. After anchoring the second horse, he headed south on the saddled horse along the wagon trail that bordered the empty railroad tracks.

"I'll bring the basket with the food," Emma said.

"We'll go on and find the perfect spot, then," Mrs. McFarland said.

With a most unladylike whoop, Penny took off in a sprint across the open valley toward the trees that lined the creek a half mile away. Dora giggled and glanced at Caroline, then grabbed her hand and tugged her along as they raced after Penny. The sight of her two new friends suddenly letting themselves have a moment of fun lightened Emma's spirit.

"I may stroll along the creek a bit before bringing the basket," Emma told Mrs. McFarland.

The older woman nodded. "A moment alone can do a body wonders." She pulled the horse from his anchor and led him along as she followed the girls at a more stately pace.

Alone, Emma walked slowly back to the wagon. Here, without anyone else around, the valley felt massive, as if the grass and sage went on and on and the mountains themselves were hundreds of miles away. A chickadee chirped its tune while a magpie insisted everyone know its presence. Mr. McFarland had told her their names one evening over dinner.

The sun warmed Emma from head to toe. She relished the time by herself. After what had happened to her at the creek, it had taken a couple of days before she could return without company. Even then, she moved quickly, turning her head this way and that and starting at every noise. There had been no more incidents. It gave her confidence, and while she still wasn't entirely at ease visiting the creek alone, she was grateful to enjoy these few moments to herself again.

She unfastened and pulled off the shrug that matched her blue and violet dress. It was the nicest dress she'd brought with her, the others being simpler day dresses and a travel dress. It was just as well, since most days she wore the Gilbert Company uniform from morning till night. She leaned over the tilted wagon and draped the shrug over one of the bench seats before removing her hat. Then she rummaged under the driver's seat for the basket of food Mrs. McFarland had packed. It was stuck against the far side of the buckboard, held firmly in place thanks to a piece of wood that connected the seat to the floor. With a determined sigh, Emma pulled off her gloves and laid them on top of her shrug. Then she hoisted up her skirts in a manner she would never do had anyone been watching, and climbed carefully into the wagon, pulling herself up by the front seat. She yanked on the basket. It didn't budge. She tried again and again. The basket refused to move.

"By jiminy," she whispered, then blushed immediately. But that was ridiculous—no one was around to hear her say it. "Jiminy!" she said, louder, as she leaned down on her hands and knees to better reach the basket.

"I hadn't pegged you as a woman who curses, Miss Daniels." A male voice came from nowhere.

Emma smacked her head on the edge of the seat as she tried to jump up. She fought the urge to say something even more scandalous than *jiminy* as she rubbed the bruise.

"I most certainly am no such thing." She winced again as she sank onto the wagon seat and turned to see the man attached to the familiar voice.

Monroe Hartley. Of course it was he who had to catch her in such a compromising position.

He reined his horse in closer to the wagon. "What happened to McFarland?"

Out of habit, Emma peered around him. Mrs. McFarland and the other girls were nowhere in sight, presumably disappeared behind the trees by the creek. Emma relaxed just a little, until she remembered who she was talking to—and how he'd come to her grateful rescue just a few days ago.

And how he made her heart beat faster and tied her tongue.

And how she should *not* be alone with him, particularly with Mrs. McFarland nearby. Although Mrs. McFarland didn't strike her to be nearly as strict as Mrs. Ruby.

Her hands twisted together in her lap, a nervous habit Mama had always warned her against. She was acutely aware of her gloves, hat, and shawl lying next to her instead of where they should be. She set a hand on either side against the bench to steady her nerves and decided it couldn't hurt to simply have a regular, polite conversation with Mr. Hartley. After all, what was she supposed to do? Ignore him and run off to the creek? That would be most impolite. No one could hold it against her to stay here and tell him what had happened.

She filled him in on the broken wheel, Mr. McFarland journeying back to Crest Stone to fix it, and the fact that they were all stuck here for a few hours. "But none of us mind too badly at all. In fact, we're all eager for a restful afternoon by the creek."

She probably should have stopped after she gave him the facts of the situation, but something compelled her to tell him more now that they were finally alone, with no immediate threat of Mrs. Ruby looming over them and packing Emma straight back to Louisville. It was almost as if she couldn't stop the words as they fell from her mouth. "The work has been more difficult than any of us expected. Of course, it won't be nearly as much once the new hotel is ready and others have arrived to handle the cleaning and the rooms and the cooking. But we have to know how to do everything because Mrs. Ruby is counting on us to train the new girls when they arrive, and to help out with training the maids and cooks and everyone else who comes to work at the hotel." She stopped to catch her breath.

Mr. Hartley nodded, and to her relief, he didn't laugh. He seemed so prone to wit, she worried she might provide some without intending such. Instead, he threw a leg over his dappled gray horse and leaped to the ground, his well-worn brown boots landing in the sandy dirt. Emma sat still as an owl on the seat, her hands clutching the bench. Her head pounded from where she had smacked it earlier, and Mr. Hartley's presence did nothing to steady it.

He tied the horse's reins around the wagon tongue. As his horse nickered and snuffed at the tufts of grass, Mr. Hartley strode the few steps to the wagon box, a mere foot or so from where Emma sat perched in Mrs. McFarland's seat.

He leaned against the side of the box and studied Emma as she turned to watch him.

She fought the urge to lower her eyes. She should dissuade him from looking at her so. But instead, her breath caught hard in her throat and she met his gaze. Finally, when she thought she might burst from anticipation, he cleared his throat and shifted, laying one hand on the edge of her seat.

"I can imagine how happy you and the other girls are to have an afternoon to relax," he said. "Now, tell me what you were doing when I rode up. Or do you have a penchant for climbing about wagons?"

Emma laughed, but it came out squeaky. What was it about this man that made her so nervous one minute and unable to stop speaking the next? She could only imagine how she had looked as he'd ridden up. She smoothed the front of her dress as she searched for the words to explain. "I . . . I was searching for our picnic basket. It's caught under the seat here." She pointed below her.

In one swift motion, he pulled himself up into the broken buckboard. Emma twisted sideways to allow him by her, but even after he passed, he was so close that she could hardly breathe.

"Pardon me," he said, a bit too late.

Emma nodded, swallowed hard, and tried to recollect her wits. Mr. Hartley knelt on the floor of the wagon and the top half of him disappeared under the seat. She looked everywhere but at him as he worked to free the basket. The bright sky, the snowcapped mountains in the distance, the clumps of trees hiding the creek, the grasshopper on the ground below, the railroad tracks and wagon trail that led into the horizon toward the house and the half-built hotel.

"Aha!" He emerged, basket in hand.

"Thank you," Emma said. "The girls will be grateful you freed their meal."

He climbed down from the wagon, and basket in one hand, he held the other out to Emma. She hesitated, realizing that not only had she taken her own gloves off, he'd removed his when he'd gotten off his horse.

He is merely being a gentleman, she told herself. Then she rested her hand in his. It was warm and a little calloused from his work, but when he wrapped his fingers around hers to hold her steady as she left the wagon, she felt the way she had when he'd rescued her from that man by the creek. Safe.

It was almost as if, with that one brief touch of skin, he promised to protect her from anything that might harm her. Emma reveled in the feeling, and when he let go, she almost gasped with the sudden loss that flooded through her.

"Are you feeling well?" he asked, his mouth curving up just a little at one corner.

"I am, thank you." Although that was quite the opposite, and she knew from that half smile he gave her that he knew it too. The man was far too confident in his effect on her. She busied herself with smoothing her skirt and collecting her hat. Her attraction to Mr. Hartley was undeniable, but she needed to keep it to herself. It was no use letting him believe she held any interest in his advances. She couldn't.

Emma paused in the midst of retying the ribbon that held her hat to her head. What if he felt nothing for her at all? What if he was simply being kind? That thought filled her with dread, even as she *knew* it shouldn't matter at all.

"Shall I leave you to your picnic?" he asked, one hand on his horse's reins.

Emma clutched the handle of the basket in both hands. "Thank you again for your help. Today and . . . last time." She glanced toward the trees, giving herself time to piece words together. "Perhaps you can tell me whether the creek is more scenic to the north or to the south? I had planned to take a short stroll along the banks before joining the girls."

Mr. Hartley turned to survey the land. He pointed to a tall hill that rose from the ground a short distance away, to the south. "That hill is a climb, but the view from the top is truly incredible. And then there is a shortcut down the back side of it to the creek, but it's easy to miss. Perhaps I could accompany you?" He took his hat into his hands and added, "So you don't get lost."

Emma's entire body went warm even as her heart ratcheted up like some kind of factory machine. She should say no, absolutely. Under no circumstances should she let herself be alone with a man—particularly this man—not only for her position as a Gilbert Girl but for her reputation.

Her eyes traced his face. That teasing look he usually wore when he spoke with her was gone. In its place was something so earnest and honest, it brought to mind how she'd felt when he'd taken her hand just a few minutes ago. Safety. Trust. She could trust him, not only with her honor, but with her life.

Feeling distinctly like Penny, Emma pondered the possibility of getting caught. It was quite low. She'd come out here for adventure, after all, in addition to supporting her family. What would it hurt to let a little of that adventure into her life now? All she had to do was keep her wits about her.

A broad smile crossing her face, Emma nodded. "Thank you. That would be most welcome."

Chapter Twelve

As he led Miss Daniels toward the hill, Monroe waffled between two warring emotions—utter happiness that she wanted him to accompany her, and sheer annoyance at his own stupidity. By the time they reached the base of the hill, the former had won him over. There was very little chance anyone would see them. They had opted to climb the hill from the south side, away from the wagon and the stretch of creek where Miss Daniels' friends rested. Even if Mrs. McFarland or one of Miss Daniels' friends returned to the wagon and saw his horse, he could easily explain that he had happened upon the empty wagon and went off looking for its occupants.

He held the picnic basket in one hand as Miss Daniels told him about the work she'd done at the house. By her account, it was a wonder she had any energy left at all for a walk, much less a climb up a hill of this size. But she showed no sign of slowing down, and easily kept up with his pace. He watched her as she climbed and talked, wondering how he had managed to meet a woman like her out on this empty frontier. It was the last thing he'd expected when he convinced Gilbert to give him the job.

"How did you arrive here?" he asked, voicing his thoughts when she paused in her account of doing laundry in a place that didn't have a water pump.

Miss Daniels laughed, and Monroe thought it was quite possibly one of the most beautiful sounds he had ever heard.

"On the train, silly," she said. "Like everyone else. And then a wagon south."

"No," he said, and he was certain he was grinning like an idiot. "I meant *why*. Why are you here, rather than with your family back in Louisville?"

She stopped and grasped onto the trunk of a lodgepole pine, one of several in a small stand that stood alone on this side of the hill. The spindly tree tilted under her grip. It was the first indication she needed a rest. Monroe stopped across from her and waited.

She looked through the trees, up toward the top of the hill, but her mind was somewhere far away. For a moment, he wished he could take back his question. Perhaps she thought him too intrusive. But then she began to speak.

"My father died several years ago. We all loved him so. He thought ahead and left us enough to live on, for a while. He was young, and his death was sudden, so we knew he'd planned to save up more for us." Her hand drifted down the tree's trunk until it was at her side. "There is still some money left, but not enough. Not for our home and the expenses of living. Not for my mother's medical condition. My mother and my sisters and brother are moving to a small apartment, but after a few months, even that will become difficult to afford."

"I'm sorry," Monroe said, at a loss for words that could truly express how much her sadness resonated with him.

"Don't be." She squared her shoulders and smiled at him, back in the present. "I miss my family, but I am grateful to have found this opportunity. My earnings from the Gilbert Company will go back to my family. And truthfully . . . ." She drifted off and twisted her bare hands together.

Monroe raised an eyebrow. "Truthfully?" She couldn't let it go at that.

Her smile grew even wider. "I wanted an adventure. I wanted more than to grow into an old maid without ever having seen anyplace outside the one where I'd grown up. I wanted more than our lovely brick house in its fashionable neighborhood off of Broadway. I wanted to see the West and meet new people and . . . well." Her face grew red, and he wondered what the last part of that sentence was meant to be.

"My father died too. And my mother," he said, by way of changing the subject away from her embarrassment. "My mother when I was eight, from illness. And my father when I was sixteen."

Miss Daniels reached out and touched his arm. It was a gesture meant to comfort, but instead the heat of her small hand burned through his shirt sleeve, stirring up the desire for him to take it in his own and pull her close to him. He didn't dare move.

"I lost my sister too." He didn't know what possessed him to say it, but he did. Something about Miss Daniels invited confidence.

Her eyes widened. "What happened?"

He kicked at a stone. He'd never felt so alone as he did when he lost Lizzie, particularly since that was his fault too.

"You don't have to say if it pains you too much," Miss Daniels said quietly.

He glanced down at her. Her face was pure empathy. Ever since Colette, he hadn't spoken of his sister to anyone else. He rubbed at his chin, and he knew Miss Daniels would keep his confidence. And perhaps she wouldn't blame him for what had happened, even if he knew otherwise. "After my father's death, I took a job on a ranch outside the city. Elizabeth—I always called her Lizzie—came with me. She was fifteen. The owner of the ranch was kind enough to let us stay in a small cabin on the edge of the property. After a while, she began keeping company with one of the other ranch hands. I wasn't happy about it—she was awfully young and he wasn't the marrying sort. She needed a mother, and that wasn't something I could be for her. I came back to the cabin one evening, and she was gone. She'd left a note that they'd run off to California and would be married."

Miss Daniels was quiet for a moment. "Surely she's written to you since then?"

Monroe shook his head. If only she had—at least he'd know she was alive. "I've never heard from her. I stayed on that ranch a year longer than we—than I—wished, only in case she sent a letter. But she never did."

"I'm so sorry." Miss Daniels squeezed his arm and he placed his free hand over hers. She stilled. "Mr. Hartley?"

"Call me Monroe, please." The familiarity felt natural as it rolled off his tongue. And out here, on the side of this hill miles from Crest Stone and everything that might keep them apart there, it felt much less dangerous.

She smiled again, and her face tinged pink. It fascinated him. There wasn't much he had ever said to Colette that made her blush. She was used to the ways of cowboys and ranch hands, having been raised around them. Not for the first time, he wondered if that was why he'd thought she'd survive the life he'd chosen, conveniently ignoring every other aspect of her personality. That gaping loss crept in again, threatening to overtake the happiness he felt at having Miss Daniels' hand under his own.

"Then you may call me Emma," she said, softly.

"Emma." He liked the way her name felt against his lips. "It suits you."

She ducked her head, and he laughed. "The way you blush at the most innocent things almost makes me want to see what happens when I say something truly scandalous."

Her face went deep scarlet at that. He wanted to wrap his fingers through hers, more than anything. His fingers twitched on top of her hand at the thought, but he didn't. He wasn't courting her—he couldn't. So instead, he smiled at her and said, "Do you think you can reach the top?"

She glanced up the hill, squared her shoulders, and shot him a fierce look. "I can, and I dare you to keep up with me." With that, she was off, sprinting up the hill while he stared after her, wondering if he would ever discover how many layers there were to this woman.

Chapter Thirteen

Her lungs squeezed as her heart pounded and her legs burned. But Emma was determined to prove she was no simpering girl from back East. Something about Mr. Hartley—Monroe—made her want him to see her as a woman strong enough to survive out here. He was right behind her, and though she suspected he held back, that didn't stop her from pushing forward even harder.

She crested the top of the hill, perspiration dotting her forehead and her hat slipping dangerously to the side. Thankfully she'd left her shawl and her gloves on the wagon. But none of her dismay mattered because the view was simply unbelievable.

"You drive a hard race, Miss Emma Daniels." Monroe rested his hands on his thighs as he leaned over to catch his breath.

"I like a challenge." She gestured around at the view. "I've never seen anything like this." The entire valley sprawled out below her. At the very edge of the horizon toward the southwest, she spotted smoke. "Is that the hotel?"

Monroe squinted into the distance and nodded. "It is." He pointed to the snowcapped mountains on their right. "Those mountains there—the Sangre de Cristos—go all the way to New Mexico. And beyond those—the Wet Mountains"—he pointed in the opposite direction, toward the smaller mountains—"are plains that stretch on and on to the east."

Emma sucked in her breath at the sheer majesty of each range of mountains—one tall and proud, and the other smooth and worn. They reminded her of a young girl showing off a new dress, and an older woman content in something plain but comfortable. How did it come to be that she found herself in such a beautiful place? God must have truly been looking out for her when she decided to brave the threat of rain for an interview over the flower shop. She turned all the way around, trying to see as much as she could. Down below, cottonwoods, willows, and aspen were thick enough to cover the creek. She couldn't even see the water, much less her friends.

"I wish we could remain here all day." When she looked at Monroe, he was already watching her, that intense warm look back in his eyes, the one that made her fingers tingle and her legs so shaky she wasn't certain she could hold herself up.

"As do I." He held her gaze as he spoke.

She swallowed, uncertain what to say next. She'd had little experience in the art of gaining and holding a man's attention. Other girls had always been so much more adept at it that Emma had usually shied into the background at home. The only one who had really paid her much attention was old Mr. Eddins, and she attempted to make any time she'd spent with him as short as possible. Perhaps she should have paid more attention to Lily. Her younger sister had always been the star of every party, before their financial situation had caused the invitations to disappear.

Not that she should be trying to gain Monroe's affections at all. But all the rules seemed so far away right now, and he was so close. The idea made her feel almost lightheaded, just as she needed to keep her head about her.

She looked away from him and forced herself to breathe normally. The mountains on either side of them remained steady, anchored to the earth. The ground of the hill underneath her held its place. She imagined herself a part of all of it, rooted to the earth, and the blood pumping through her veins slowed to almost normal. Only then did she trust herself to glance back at Monroe.

He was watching her still, which instead of making her go warm all over in embarrassment, was almost comforting. She gave him a warm smile, and his face lit up as if she'd offered him the entire valley below them. The quiet, the scenery, the presence of the man next to her . . . Now that she could breathe, Emma had never felt more at peace than she did right here on this hill with Monroe. Neither of them spoke, but it didn't matter.

A poem began to form in her head. She worked around the words, letting them settle where they best seemed to fit. And then she sat, pulling her book and a worn bit of pencil from the small bag that hung from her dress.

"Emma?" Monroe sounded puzzled, but Emma didn't have a moment to look up, not if she wanted to get these words down before they disappeared from her head altogether. Words were like fog on a damp morning—all-encompassing but destined to slip away.

She wasn't certain how long she sat among the stones and dirt and bushy piles of sage, scratching out the lines. But finally, she finished. Smiling at her work, she stood slowly and let the world come back to her.

"I confess, I'm curious about what you wrote. I'm beginning to believe it's a poem about a dashing young man standing among the peaks and valley." Monroe gave her a grin that made her laugh from the very core of herself.

"I hate to disappoint you. But the mountains do play a role." She rolled the pencil between her fingers. She'd never shared her poetry with anyone except Lily, but some strange force made her tear the page from her book and hand it to Monroe.

He blinked at her a moment, as if he disbelieved she'd chosen him, but she nodded, and his eyes went to the page in his hand. Emma waited, turning her book over and over in her hands, fearing with each second that he'd find her a fraud, a silly girl with a head full of clouds who masqueraded as some serious poet to while away the time.

Finally, he looked up at her. Then back at the page. "This bit here, about loneliness and longing for the way the peaks touch the sky—"

She cringed a little, hearing him echo her sentiments. "They're yours. The words."

A soft smile lit up his face. "I can't believe you used them. I was teasing you about that."

"They worked. And they're quite lovely, I think."

He glanced down again. "The entire poem is lovely. May I keep it?"

She nodded even as her face went warm at the thought of him rereading her words later, when he was alone.

The light had shifted a bit to the west, lengthening the shadows. Despite never wanting to leave this spot, she knew they needed to return down the other side, or she'd risk one of the girls coming to search for her.

Almost as if reading her mind, Monroe leaned forward and picked up the basket. "I don't wish to leave, but your friends will begin to worry."

She nodded and followed him across the top of the hill, toward the west side where it would meet the creek below. Watching his back, she promised herself she would remember everything about this afternoon for the rest of her life—the way the breeze lifted the tendrils of hair that framed her face, the song of the birds in the trees below, the still and cloudless sky, the never-changing mountains protecting both sides of their valley, how safe her hand felt under his, the way he looked at her as if she were everything he'd ever wanted in the world. Emma wished she could frame the moment like a photograph and hold it close to her heart. If only it could be like this forever, but she knew that would never be.

Halfway down the hill, one bird called louder than the rest. Emma turned to Monroe, puzzled. Until it called again.

"Penny!" Emma stopped short.

"She must've grown impatient," Monroe said.

Thoughts raced through her head. If Penny saw them . . . She'd likely be delighted, but Penny loved to talk. Emma wasn't certain how good she'd be at keeping secrets.

Monroe reached up and grazed his fingers across Emma's jaw. For the briefest moment, all thoughts of Penny and losing her position at the hotel flew from Emma's mind. All that existed was her and Monroe and the feel of his hand against her face. Out of some instinct she never knew existed, she leaned into his touch. He smiled at her, then dropped his hand and held out the basket.

Emma swayed a little without the strength of his calloused touch against her face. She took the basket, and it felt as if she were falling back to Earth without even a net to catch her.

"I'll see you soon?"

The way he phrased it like a question was more than enough to melt her like a bit of chocolate in the sun. She nodded, ignoring all the better judgment she'd ever had. "Thank you for today."

His smile lit up his entire face. He tipped his hat at her, then he was gone, around toward the south side of the hill.

"Emma! Are you up there?"

Emma glanced behind her one last time. Monroe was gone. She turned and took a few steps down the hill before she answered Penny. "Coming!"

"Oh, thank goodness." Penny appeared just past a large pine tree. She stopped and grabbed on to the trunk. "I believe this sort of exertion might do me in." She looked Emma up and down. "Whatever possessed you to go up this hill?"

"The view," Emma said easily. It was the truth, just without the part about the handsome man who had convinced her the view was worthwhile.

Penny reached for the basket and peeked inside. "I was certain you'd run off and had our entire meal by yourself." When she looked up again, her green eyes sparkled, and Emma couldn't help but laugh.

"You are truly the least trusting person I've ever met," Emma teased.

"Not at all! Just hungry." Penny looped her arm through Emma's, and they started their way down the hill again. "Dora was afraid you'd been hurt, and Caroline thought an Indian warrior had come and swept you off your feet. For such a demure girl, she has quite the imagination. I'm surprised I didn't think of that one first."

Penny talked about how they had already put their feet in the creek and nearly froze, then about Mrs. McFarland's stories of being courted by Mr. Mc-Farland in the moving railroad town that had come before them in Crest Stone, and about anything else that crossed her mind as they moved down the hill and then along the creek. Emma nodded here and there, but mostly she was grateful not to have to contribute to the conversation.

Monroe occupied her mind, and she wasn't certain if she could ever get him out.

Chapter Fourteen

Monroe yawned and rubbed at his freshly-shaved chin. He stood next to the tracks in his only suit and boots that had been shined within an inch of their lives, when all he really wanted was a long night's rest in his tent. The past week had been grueling. Earlier in the week, another train had arrived from Cañon City, not carrying passengers yet as there was still no terminus in Santa Fe, but instead, a load of cut lumber, factory-made nails, shingles, powder for making plaster, and any number of construction supplies, all of which his crew had been running short on. With the delivery was a message from Mr. Gilbert—he was coming with company investors in one week's time to see the progress on the hotel.

Since then, Monroe and his crew had worked nearly nonstop, from before sunrise to after sunset. He was pleased with the progress they'd made, and he only hoped the company would agree. The place actually looked like it might be a habitable building in a month's time. It had floors, a roof, and almost every room had been walled in. They had nearly decimated the shipment that had been sent a week ago. As he stood near the tracks with Turner and Big Jim, he prayed the train that pulled up now carried wood, nails, more doors, and glass for windows.

Just as the train squealed to a stop in front of him, Monroe caught a glimpse of a blue and violet dress on the other side of the tracks. His breath caught in his throat and he coughed. Big Jim slapped him on the back. He hadn't seen Emma from more than a distance since their excursion up the hill, five miles north of here, a week and a half ago. She was the last thing he thought of every night and first thing he pictured each morning, though. With a start, he realized that while he still dreamed of Colette here and there, that aching loneliness hadn't reared its ugly head since that Sunday he'd found McFarland's wagon. Was that Emma's doing?

"You're grinning like a fool," Big Jim muttered as the engine let out a puff of steam.

Monroe tried to wipe it from his face as he realized Turner was watching him too. He needed to focus. His business was on the line here. If Mr. Gilbert and the investors were pleased, not only would he be able to stay on to finish his work and earn the promised bonus, they'd give him an excellent reference. Perhaps Gilbert might even ask him to build another hotel.

The door to the first car opened, and when the steam cleared, Monroe spotted several men and one woman now standing beside the tracks. Big Jim wished him luck before returning to check on the crew. Monroe moved forward, Turner on his heels, to greet them.

"Ah! Here is our intrepid builder, Mr. Monroe Hartley." Gilbert went around the circle and made introductions.

As Monroe shook hands with each investor, he spotted another several cars behind the first. He turned to Gilbert, ready to ask if they might be filled with supplies, when Gilbert did the answering for him.

"Everything you need for a couple more weeks, I dare hope!" He clapped Monroe on the back.

Turner cleared his throat. Monroe gave him a pointed look before introducing his foreman to Gilbert and the investors. Turner shook their hands, and Monroe had to admire how professional the man was, despite his impatience.

"I think you'll be pleased with what we've done." Turner gestured at the hotel. "I told Hartley we ought to be onto the interior woodwork by now, so I hope you'll forgive us for being behind."

His words nearly knocked Monroe upside the head. That was beyond an eagerness to learn. What would possess him to say something like that? Here they were, with the structure of an entire hotel nearly completed in the span of six weeks, and Turner seemed to be trying to make them look as if they were behind schedule—when in truth, they were ahead. For the life of him, Monroe couldn't figure out why. Did the man not want his portion of the bonus?

Gilbert furrowed his brows before letting his usual businessman's confidence reclaim his face. "Still, what Hartley and the men have achieved so far is nothing short of miraculous."

Turner opened his mouth to speak again, but this time Monroe beat him to it. "Mr. Turner needs to get back to the men. After all, we must ensure this hotel is completed on time." Before the foreman could protest, Monroe caught his eye and said, "Thank you for taking this time away from your work. We all know how lost the crew is without you. I appreciate you keeping them in line." They'd need to have a conversation later. Monroe couldn't let those remarks go unchecked.

Turner pressed his lips together. Then he nodded at Gilbert and the others and headed up the hill toward the hotel.

After a bit more small talk, Gilbert asked, "Shall we tour what you've completed so far?"

"Right this way." Monroe led the group up the hill and across the open valley to where the new hotel sat. The crew was hard at work, unseen from outside as they plastered the walls on the second floor. They didn't have time to lose, not to mention he didn't want Gilbert or the investors to think they were easing off work simply because they had guests.

"You've made a lot of progress since I was here last," Gilbert said, his voice breathy with the exertion of the walk.

Monroe slowed down some. Spending every day outside at work, he'd forgotten how some men might not be up to the effort of such a vigorous stroll. "We've put in extra hours each day for the past week. My goal is to have this building completed ahead of schedule." He couldn't hide the pride in his voice. He wanted Gilbert to know he'd hired the best for this job.

And by the look on Gilbert's face, he had succeeded. The man's eyes widened as they arrived at the building. "The walls are finished, too?"

"Just about. As of this morning, there were only a few on the second floor that needed plaster. That's what the men are working on now. We even have a few doors—the ones that arrived in the last shipment—hung." Monroe put both hands on his hips and turned to see what the investors thought.

But it wasn't the investors who caught his eye. A group of six women had arrived at the rear of the crowd, all dressed in their finest. Their number included one radiant young woman in a blue and purple dress and swoops of dark hair pinned up under a matching hat. The same hat that had slid down her escaping hair when they'd climbed a hill together over a week ago. Her eyes turned to Monroe, and he wondered if he would burst into flames on the spot.

"Pardon me, Mr. Gilbert, Mr. Hartley." McFarland appeared from behind the women. "I thought these fine gentlemen and lady might like to meet the Crest Stone Hotel's staff and the first group of Gilbert Girls."

"We would indeed," the lady investor said as Monroe and the other men in the group removed their hats. "I do love how you employ young women, Mr. Gilbert. There are few opportunities in this world for ladies to support their families in positions of meaning and worth." She turned to speak to Emma and the other girls. "I admire your bravery in venturing out to this wilderness to add a touch of civility and gentleness."

Emma beamed at the woman. Her smile reached every inch of Monroe. She was a strongly independent woman under all of her manners and good graces. While that might deter some men, it intrigued him. Colette had held similar qualities—at least while they'd lived on her family's ranch. Maybe it was the time of day or perhaps it was the company, but the great aching loss he usually felt upon thinking of Colette was less sharp and more blurred with nostalgia.

"This is Michael McFarland," Gilbert said to the investors after he named them one by one. "He's to be the manager of the hotel. His wife, Mrs. McFarland, will do the books."

After shaking hands with the investors, McFarland picked up the introductions in his light Irish brogue. "This is Mrs. Ruby, house mother to the Crest Stone's Gilbert Girls and manager of the dining room. She comes to us from another Gilbert Company establishment north of Denver." He moved on to the girls, each of whom inclined her head as she was introduced. Monroe could barely take his eyes from Emma. She positively glowed, and he wondered how every man in the group wasn't as fixated on her as he was. This work suited her—entertaining folks, working hard. He dared to hope the Territory suited her too, much more than Kentucky.

"Quite marvelous to meet you all," the tall, thin male investor said as he held his hat in his hands. The others nodded and murmured in agreement.

"If it is not a problem, we will join you all on your tour of the new hotel," Mr. McFarland said. "The ladies have wanted to see it for quite some time now."

"I think that's a splendid idea," Gilbert said. "Hartley?"

Monroe detached his tongue from its stunned position against his upper palate and managed to speak. "That's fine by me. Shall we start at the entry?" He dragged his eyes away from Emma and led the group to what would be the front door. Reminding himself that his career depended on this tour, he swept a hand across the sage and grass-filled field in front of the door. "When all is finished, this area will have a circular drive for carriages that will be waiting for passengers at the train depot below. I believe Mr. Gilbert has plans for flowering trees and a fountain."

"Indeed!" Mr. Gilbert said. "My father and I like each of our hotels to be nearly indistinguishable from any fine establishment you might find in New York or Philadelphia."

The investors agreed this was for the best, and Monroe tightened his jaw to keep his own words to himself. It was ridiculous to plant trees that would need buckets of extra water to simply survive out here, not to mention constructing a fountain. That would require some type of plumbing system that led from the creek a quarter mile away.

He remained quiet and led the group through the entry that would eventually have two imposing doors. They emerged in the sprawling lobby area.

The group looked around, clearly impressed with the size of the room. As Gilbert explained how the area would be decorated in the usual Gilbert Company style with richly colored rugs, furs, and trophy heads on the walls, Monroe backed against what would become one of the large stone fireplaces that banked each side wall.

"Hello." A soft voice reached his ears.

He glanced down next to him, and sure enough, Emma stood there, flanking the edge of her group of ladies. He smiled in a way that he hoped was not the least bit suspicious to anyone else watching. What he wouldn't give for a moment alone with her right now. It had been too long since their climb up the hill. Since then, in the few waking moments he wasn't consumed by work, he almost itched to feel the softness of her cheek, hear her laugh, and have her look at him with those green eyes that he could swear saw straight through to his soul. Now here she was, barely inches from him, and he could do nothing about it.

"Hartley?" Gilbert was looking at him, waiting for him to do or say something, and Monroe had no idea what that might be.

He cleared his throat to buy time and luckily noticed a couple of the investors making their way across the room to the large openings that would be two very big doors to the dining room. He increased his stride to reach the room before them and then gestured them inside.

"As you can see, this will be the Gilbert Company's largest and finest dining room to date. The kitchen is located in the rear, and this room should hold one hundred tables once it is completed." Monroe clasped his hands behind his back and enjoyed the looks of awe from the investors.

"Will you even have that many passengers?" the lady investor asked Gilbert.

"We anticipate so," he replied. "The springs in and around Santa Fe are growing in popularity, and since the trains will only stop for about thirty minutes, we need the ability to seat all passengers who wish to eat in the dining room at once. A lunch counter for those traveling more economically will also be available." He gestured toward the lobby, with its separate entrance into the room housing the lunch counter.

"These ladies cannot possibly serve that many tables on their own," a short, squat man joked as he gestured to Emma and her friends.

"We most certainly could try," the girl with golden-brown ringlets and an infectious smile said. Miss May, Monroe remembered from the introductions.

Mrs. Ruby tensed and laid a hand on the girl's shoulder. But the group laughed after taking a moment to let her brash outburst sink in. Emma concealed a smile behind her gloved hand, and Monroe wished with all his heart that she'd laugh out loud. He needed to hear that sound almost as badly as he needed air to breathe.

"If you please, sirs, madam," Mrs. Ruby said, pushing her way in front of the outspoken girl. "Mr. Gilbert has informed me that we will gradually increase the number of Gilbert Girls on premises until there are approximately thirty girls. This will allow each girl to serve only a few tables, which will provide ample time for guests to engage them in conversation and for them to give their full attention to their customers. The last thing we want in a Gilbert dining room is a rushed, harried girl."

"That is a most excellent plan," the little round man said. "Gilbert, I commend you and your father on maintaining the company standards at each new property."

They continued with the tour. Monroe led the group to the gentlemen's lounge, the ladies' parlor, the small tearoom, the lunch counter, and what would be the outdoor garden area on the first floor, and then commenced showing a few of the guest rooms on the upper level.

Just as Monroe was explaining plans for the guest rooms, Mrs. Ruby piped up. "Where is Miss Daniels?"

Monroe paused and looked around the group. Emma was nowhere to be seen.

Chapter Fifteen

"Open, please, will you?" Emma tugged at the door again, but it wouldn't budge on its shiny brass hinges. She sighed, the air escaping her lips in an irritated huff. This was what she got for being so curious, she supposed.

She'd only wanted to see what was behind one of the few doors that had been hung in the hotel. It led to a small room just off the tearoom. Once she stepped inside, she'd shut the door—just briefly—to get a better sense for what the room might be like when it was finished. But when she turned to confirm with Monroe that it would be a powder room, she could not pry the door open. By then, the group had moved from the tearoom into the hallway. Feeling like a fool, she hadn't cried out for help. In fact, she was certain that all she needed to do was pull the door just so since it had no knob yet, and it would open again. She'd had no problems shutting it, after all.

But her assumption was clearly incorrect, and now she'd spent a good ten minutes pulling and prying at the door with no luck at all. "Hello?" she called. "Is anyone out there?"

No answer.

Of course there wouldn't be. The tour group had probably moved upstairs by now, and the workers were all up there too, finishing the walls in the guest rooms.

Emma turned behind her, searching for something she might use as a lever in the hole where the doorknob would eventually go. She'd have to free herself. Now if she could just find the right tool . . .

A few pieces of discarded wood littered the edges of the room. Perhaps one of those might work. Emma selected a thin, rectangular piece. She peeled off her gloves to keep the satin from snagging, and, careful not to place the jagged edges too near her hand, she inserted the end of the wood into the hole and pushed against the other end with all her might.

Snap! The wood splintered in the middle and Emma crashed headfirst into the door. She threw the wood to the floor, harder than any gentle lady should ever throw anything. But fie on any conventions at this moment. She was alone, her forehead throbbed, and desperation was beginning to creep into the edges of her thoughts.

She forced herself to breathe normally as she rubbed the sore spot on her forehead. Scanning the bits of wood again, she spotted one more possibility. This piece was a bit thicker, and therefore less likely to snap in two. Emma set the wood inside the hole again. It just barely fit. Gathering her lower lip between her teeth, she bore down on the wood. It held. She paused, wiped the perspiration from her aching forehead, and then leaned all of her weight into the piece of wood. The door flew open.

She stumbled forward. The wood fell from her hands. She tried to catch herself, but landed hard against something solid. Hands gripped her upper arms and stood her back upright.

Trying to catch her breath, Emma looked up.

"Monroe?" she said, between breaths.

He grinned at her. "I thought you might be down here."

"How so?" Emma tried to concentrate on what he was saying, and not the strong hands that still held her arms.

"I remembered you looking almost longingly at this door when we were in here. If I hadn't been distracted by Gilbert's insistence that future hotels have a tearoom attached to the dining room, I might've seen you disappear into here."

Emma shifted her weight, and he seemed to realize he was still holding her. He dropped his hands immediately, but he didn't take his eyes from hers. She swallowed hard, at a loss for words again.

"What do you think? Is it spacious enough for a powder room?" He slipped past her into the smaller space and held his arms out to the sides. "Although the dimensions aren't mine. I might've made it a bit larger."

Emma smiled and stepped forward, this time leaving that pesky door open. She ran her hand almost lovingly over the woodwork of the doorframe. It was one of the only completed pieces of interior woodwork, and her eyes had been drawn to it immediately. She doubted any blueprints specified the detail that went into pieces like this one. The carefully created swirls and arches in the frame were all Monroe's. "It's perfect. Or it will be, once it has tables and rugs and mirrors and a place to rest."

"Demanding, aren't you?" he teased.

"I'm no such thing! I'm simply informing a man who grew up outside the comforts of a real city how a powder room should be presented." She drew herself up straight.

"Are you saying I'm some sort of ruffian?"

She could almost hear the laughter behind his words. It made her smile even as she defended herself. "You put words in my mouth, sir. All I meant was that I should know a good powder room better than a man who grew up in the Colorado Territory."

"Uncivilized mountain man, then." He leaned against the wall, clearly enjoying this far too much.

Emma opened her mouth to retort when she became acutely aware of how alone they were, and how dangerous this situation was. She swallowed and glanced behind her. "Where is the rest of the group?"

"Mrs. McFarland and Mrs. Ruby have led the girls back outside with the investors and Mr. Gilbert. Mr. McFarland is searching for you upstairs. You gave us all quite a scare, you know." He stepped forward and swiped up the broken piece of wood from the floor. He held it up between them. "What is this?"

"My first attempt at levering the door open. It was stuck."

He tilted his head as he tossed the wood to the floor, that infernal grin crossing his face again. "Are you implying my craftsmanship is not up to your standards?"

"I'm saying I got stuck in this room through no fault of my own." She held his gaze, one hand on her hip.

He took another step forward and reached around her for the door. He pulled it shut just as she shouted, "No! You'll close us in."

"I'll do no such thing. Watch." He pushed on the door.

Nothing happened.

"See?" She looked up at him. He was but mere inches from her, so close, yet so far away.

He pushed again and cursed under his breath, so low she knew she wasn't meant to hear it. "I hung this one myself. I must've not set the hinges right."

Emma scooped up the broken piece of wood from the floor. "Lever?" She held it up in front of her face and gave him a satisfied grin.

He glanced down and laughed. Then he took the piece of wood. She expected him to do as she had and insert it into the doorknob hole. But instead, he hesitated. His left hand came up to caress her face the same way he'd done on top of the hill a week ago.

Oh, how she'd relived that moment. Over and over and over again, while cleaning dishes, while ironing dresses, while trying to sleep at night. Each time, she'd imagined the feel of his rough palm against her cheek. She'd yearned for it to happen again, all the while knowing it shouldn't.

And now it was. She should stop it, if she had any sense. But she couldn't breathe, her corset feeling even more snug around her ribcage than it usually did. Finally, she forced a ragged breath, just as his hand dropped to her jaw. Almost without thought, her own hands reached for his back and rested lightly against his coat. He stiffened for a moment, then relaxed.

His eyes held hers, reflecting tenderness. But there was something deeper, almost like lightning beneath the warmth, and it both terrified and excited her. Almost as if he knew what she saw, he smiled just a little and took a step closer.

Emma's heart pounded as his hand moved to the back of her head, just underneath the knot of hair that rested beneath the narrow brim of her hat. His fingers splayed wide, so that they covered the back of her neck. She thought she could stand here like this forever. He lowered his face, keeping his eyes on hers, and she felt pinned to this place, as if she would never move again.

"Hartley? Did you find her?"

Emma's breath burst from her throat as Monroe yanked his hand back. They each backed up, him breathing hard as she ran her hands over her face, feeling it grow warmer under her own palms.

"We're in here. Can you let us out?" Monroe finally called back, his voice pitched slightly lower than normal.

"Where—?" Mr. McFarland stopped speaking as they heard his shoes enter the room just outside the door. He pulled on the door. "How the dickens—pardon me, Miss Daniels—did this door get jammed?"

"The hinges are hung incorrectly," Monroe said. "If you can find a long enough piece of wood, you should be able to lever it open."

They heard him rummaging around until finally a long square of wood poked through the doorknob hole. "I'm going to give this a try." With a few yanks, the door finally sprung free, and Mr. McFarland stood just beyond it.

"Thank you ever so much, Mr. McFarland," Emma said, praying she looked more composed than she felt. If she looked anything like she felt, her hair would be wild, her dress a wrinkled mess, and her face as flushed as if she'd just cleaned the entire stove back at the house. She kept speaking, hoping it would hide anything that might give her true feelings away. "I'd managed to open it when Mr. Hartley arrived. He tried the door again, and, well, now he believes there is something wrong with it."

Monroe shot her a look, and she realized a split second too late that she'd perhaps said too much. Mr. McFarland glanced between them both, but said nothing beyond, "Come, let's rejoin the group." He ushered her forward.

Outside the hotel, Mrs. McFarland fussed over her while Mrs. Ruby clucked over her curiosity. Emma finally waved them all off, insisting she was fine and praising Monroe for finding her so quickly. The attention then turned to him, and even as he tried to play it off, he shot her a knowing smile. It lasted less than a second, but it made Emma wish Mr. McFarland hadn't found them. She ducked her head to hide her own smile and the warmth that crept into her face once more. She felt lost in her own world as the group moved toward the railroad tracks and the house below.

Caroline appeared by her side, slipped an arm through Emma's, and whispered, "He's like Sir Lancelot, and you are Lady Guinevere."

"Oh, hush," Emma whispered back. "It's no such thing."

"Mmmhmm." Caroline squeezed her arm but said nothing else. Emma knew Caroline would keep her confidence, thankfully.

Emma kept her eyes forward, but let them stray from time to time to Monroe's back. He was deep in conversation with one of the investors, but all she could think about was what it might have been like if he had kissed her. Just the thought nearly made her trip over nothing. What she should be thinking about was what would have happened if Mr. McFarland had caught her in Monroe's arms.

But then Monroe sent a glance her way—and a tiny smile just for her—and all sensible thoughts flew from her mind again.

He was kindness and heat and the threat of her complete undoing, and she could not stay away.

Chapter Sixteen

Long after he'd seen the investors and Gilbert off, Monroe sat by himself in front of a crackling fire near his tent. It was oddly quiet in the camp tonight. Many of the men had passed out as soon as they'd eaten, exhausted from a week of nonstop work. Big Jim and Turner had stopped by briefly to share a cup of stew and talk about tomorrow's plans to unload the freight cars. Turner had apologized for how he'd acted in front of the investors, and after that, they'd shared an easy evening. But now it was nearing ten o'clock, and only a few murmurs could be heard here and there.

He broke a twig in half and tossed the pieces into the fire, watching as the orange flames consumed them. And he thought about Emma, as he'd done ever since she'd returned to the house to serve dinner to the investors and prepare their rooms.

After Colette had died, he was sure he would never love any woman again the way he had loved her. It was impossible. A piece of his heart had gone with her, and even though two years had passed, the guilt still haunted him. If only he'd listened to her when she told him that all she wanted was a home and a garden. He'd heard her, of course, but he'd brushed her desires aside in favor of his own dreams. And it had killed her. He'd have to live with that for the rest of his life. Colette had been perfect—kind, funny, smart, and beautiful. They had connected instantly, the moment he'd said hello.

Almost the same way he and Emma had.

Was it possible?

He shook his head and stoked the fire with a limb he'd found down by the creek. It couldn't be. And even if it was, there was nothing he could do about it—not if he wanted to retain his job and keep her alive. The best thing for him to do was to remain distant from her, for her own protection.

"Can I sit a spell?"

Monroe stood fast, taken by surprise, hand reaching for the shotgun behind him.

McFarland chuckled and ran a hand over his salt-and-pepper beard. "Didn't mean to startle you."

Monroe set the shotgun down and gestured at the blanket that covered the ground. McFarland sat. They were both quiet for a few moments. McFarland took out a cigar, lit it, and puffed out smoke. Monroe waited, wondering why the man was paying a visit so late.

"Smoke?" McFarland asked, holding another cigar out to Monroe.

He declined, and McFarland pocketed it.

"Mrs. McFarland informed me that Miss Daniels was going to get an earful this evening from Mrs. Ruby."

Monroe furrowed his brows. "And why is that?"

"For letting herself be alone with you."

He chuckled, then realized McFarland was dead serious. "That's ridiculous. She did nothing wrong. *We* did nothing wrong." The lie spilled out of his mouth easily. She may not have done a thing, but he had been forward with her, and he knew it.

"I agree. It's unfortunate, but that's the way of it. Old Man Gilbert takes the virtue of his female employees a bit too seriously, I think."

The venison stew Monroe had eaten earlier churned in his stomach. Why had he been such a fool? "Will she lose her position?"

McFarland shook his head. "I doubt it. I believe Mrs. Ruby sees the situation as an unfortunate accident. She'll likely use it as a warning." He studied the end of the cigar, then glanced at Monroe. "This is supposed to be my warning to you."

Monroe pursed his lips and stared into the flames. "Does Gilbert know about this?"

"He's not aware, nor did he say anything after Miss Daniels was found."

Monroe nodded. "Thank you for your discretion."

"There's no way to lose your position faster in this company than by courting scandal. I've heard of a man up north in Montana several years back, when the elder Gilbert was just beginning to open these hotels. He was working as a clerk in the hotel, and he had the audacity to take one of the girls out to a church service, of all things, but with no chaperone. He was gone the next day,

and I heard no other hotel would hire him after that. No decent hotel, that is."
McFarland stood. "Well, I best get back before the missus comes a-looking for
me."

Monroe said good night and watched as the older man made his way back
down to the rickety old railroad shanty that served as his home. Long after Mc-
Farland had disappeared into the darkness, Monroe still sat, watching the lights
in the larger house go off one by one until only one remained alight in the third-
floor garret. Was that Emma's? Perhaps she was still awake, thoughts churning
the way his did.

More than anything, he wanted to go to her. Hold her and tell her it would
all be okay. No one would ever make her leave her work, unless she wanted to
go. But that would be a lie, as they'd both found out tonight. He'd lose the one
thing that kept his mind off everything he'd already lost in his life. He couldn't
afford to let anything like this happen again.

But what kept him up, eyes on the last light in the house, was the nagging
feeling that he wasn't certain if he was prepared to lose Emma in exchange.

Chapter Seventeen

It was nearing eleven o'clock when they dried the last dish and swept the last crumb from the floor. Emma was slipping into sleep where she stood. She wasn't entirely certain how she would even be able to climb the stairs in such a tired state, never mind put to paper the poem that had been forming in her head for hours while she worked. It felt like one of her best, the right words flitting into her mind and knitting themselves together as she scrubbed dishes and floors and as she waited to bring the investors more coffee and pastries. Once the words turned from wisps of idea into ink, the intense feelings she had for Monroe might leave her alone for a few moments and allow her to concentrate on her work.

The investors and Mr. Gilbert had finally turned in an hour ago. Since then, Emma and the other girls had worked nonstop to put the kitchen and dining room back to rights and prepare for the morning's breakfast. Grateful to finally have the work done, especially considering how her mind had been mostly elsewhere for the evening, Emma followed the other girls out of the kitchen and toward the stairs.

"Emma? May I have a word?" Mrs. Ruby stood at the foot of the stairs.

Emma nodded, tucking away her disappointment at not immediately getting to set her words on paper. When the last of the girls had disappeared up the stairs, Mrs. Ruby led Emma to a small office at the rear of the house. Emma had only been in here once, to fetch a pair of scissors for Mrs. Ruby. Now, she sat in the stiff-backed chair across from the desk while Mrs. Ruby settled herself on the opposite side. She sat up straight, ever the model of decorum.

Emma followed suit, even though her back ached. She folded her hands and waited impatiently.

"I know you are a girl from a good family," Mrs. Ruby started. "And I doubt you had any ill intentions this afternoon, but I must tell you that it is unacceptable for you to be found unaccompanied with a man."

Emma's throat went dry. Her fingers began to tremble, and she held them tightly together to try to make them stop.

"By pure chance, none of the investors saw the situation, and you've been nothing but a shining example of what a Gilbert Girl should be up until now. Therefore, you may keep your position here. But you must consider this a warning. Any further infractions will result in your immediate dismissal. Do you understand?"

"Yes . . . yes, I understand." Emma could hardly keep her voice from shaking. She'd come so close to losing the one thing she needed—security for her family—and the one thing she wanted above all else—her own independence. All for what? A moment's curiosity? "It was a happenstance. I apologize."

"I know." Mrs. Ruby's eyes softened. "And I'm sorry I had to do this."

"It will never happen again," Emma promised. She prayed she could keep that promise. She *had* to, no matter her feelings about Monroe.

But would she take back those short, sweet moments they'd shared together if she could? She wasn't sure. In fact, her mind had wandered so far tonight that while she was scrubbing the roast pan, she'd fully imagined herself scrubbing her own pan in her own home while Monroe went out to tend to the horses. When she'd realized what she was doing, she'd almost laughed out loud.

Now, she squeezed her eyes shut briefly. She knew it was foolish, imagining that a few stolen moments would lead to a life together. And even if it could, would it actually happen? Could she leave her work? Her heart thumped wildly at the mere thought, but then her brain took over. Even if she was willing to lose the independence she had craved so badly at home and had found here, she couldn't afford to resign from her position as a Gilbert Girl. She couldn't ask a man who had never even met her family to send them money each month. And even if she could, where would that money come from? As soon as Monroe would make his intentions known, Mr. Gilbert would fire him, and he would have no income.

But even with all of those arguments against it, even as presumptuous as it was to assume Monroe was of the same mind, Emma couldn't help but wish Mr.

McFarland had never found them. That she was still alone with Monroe in that little room. That he'd moved one step closer . . .

With a sigh, Emma shook the thoughts from her head. She shouldn't be thinking such things. She was in a precarious situation, and she needed to keep her wits about her.

Mrs. Ruby handed her an off-white envelope. Confused, Emma took it.

"Remember what I said. Now go on upstairs and read your letter." Mrs. Ruby reached for the lamp she'd set down on the desk and handed it to Emma. "I'll find another lamp in the kitchen." She smiled.

Taking the lamp and saying good night to Mrs. Ruby, Emma paused just outside her door and glanced at the envelope. Her name, with the name of the hotel and Crest Stone, Colorado Territory underneath, were neatly written on the front. Joy at seeing her sister's handwriting erased all embarrassment from Mrs. Ruby's warning and confusion about her feelings for Monroe. Emma hurried through the house and up the stairs. Inside the big attic room she shared with the other girls, she found the lamp they'd taken still burning and not a soul awake. Laughing quietly to herself, Emma moved to extinguish the other lamp. Penny lay facedown on the bed she shared with Emma, having not even removed her work dress or apron. Caroline had fallen asleep without taking her hair down, and Dora was curled up in a tight ball, her shoes still on.

Quietly, Emma sat in the chair that flanked a small dressing table on the far side of the room. Not having a letter opener, she slid her dishwater-reddened finger into the crease of the envelope to open it. She'd sent a letter home each week, but this was the first she'd had in return. The money she'd sent should be arriving soon, if it hadn't already. Eager for news from home, Emma flattened the letter on the table and moved the lamp closer to read her sister's small handwriting.

My dearest Emma,

I hope this letter finds you well and enjoying all of the opportunities your new position has to offer. I apologize for not writing sooner, but I hate to burden you with our troubles. It is dreary here at home. Outside, it is beautiful—the days are warm and the sun shines more often than not. But inside . . . Oh Emma. I don't know what we will do. I know you're sending money, and we wait patiently for it.

Just yesterday, Mama's physician insisted we pay him what he was owed or he would no longer treat her. And she was in such pain, that I did the only thing I could. *I went to the bank and withdrew the last of Papa's funds—the money we intended to use to pay for this apartment for the next few months. I gave it all to the doctor, and it took care of what we owed. He gave Mama some medicine, and now she feels much better. But we are done for. We have nothing left. Grace and I have decided to take on some sewing. It won't be much, but we pray it will be enough to keep the landlord happy while we wait for your wages. If it isn't, then we will find work at a factory. The lady and her daughter who live in the rooms next to ours work at a garment manufacturer. Perhaps the owner of that establishment will take us on.*

Please write and tell us of your adventures. Your stories will keep us strong even in these dark times.

Your loving sister,

Lillian

Emma read the letter again, hoping the words would change, but they didn't. Her soul felt empty, not only because she missed her dear sister and their family, but because she felt she could do nothing. The money she'd sent had to arrive before things grew too desperate for her family. Maybe it was already there. The last thing she wanted was her sisters working in a garment factory, spending long hours hunched over in the dim light and growing wan and thin.

She brushed away the tears that had started falling. She had no desire to write that poem down now, not after Lily's letter. If she tried to write now, it wouldn't be carefully chosen words about her feelings for Monroe; it would be about the fear that stirred deep inside her.

If it weren't for this work, she'd be helpless. Her entire family would be destitute, and their only salvation would be factory work. Emma pressed the letter to her chest, almost as if she could feel her sister inside of it. The money would arrive soon, and it would be enough to keep them until she could send more. They were her responsibility. It was up to her to keep them safe and her sisters free from the dangers that came with factory work.

She folded the letter, slid it back into its envelope, and tucked it into the pocket of her best dress that hung from a peg on the wall. Then she quickly undressed, relishing that first full breath after unlacing her corset, and blew out the lamp.

Before she sank into bed next to Penny, she stood at the window that over-looked the new hotel and the camp. Here and there, a fire burned among the tents. Monroe was out there, somewhere. She wondered if he thought of her.

She closed her eyes. Tonight had made one thing clear—she could have peace of mind for her family, or she could have Monroe.

She couldn't have both.

Chapter Eighteen

In the week since the investors had left, Monroe had been more than busy, directing his crew to hang doors, add glass to windows, and place siding. Yet, despite the work and despite the subtle warning McFarland had given him and despite his own sense, he still took detours by the house, hoping to spot Emma.

But each time, she was nowhere to be found or disappeared the second he laid eyes on her. He'd even ridden north on Sunday again, wondering if they might stop for another picnic. He'd ended up watching from a distance as the wagon bounced its way past the hill he'd climbed with Emma.

In the back of his mind, he knew it was for the best. Emma was being smarter than he. He only wished she'd at least look at him. What he would give for one more moment with her. He'd ask to hear more of her poetry. He'd take her hand again. He'd . . .

Perhaps it was a good thing they hadn't crossed paths in a week.

He ran an arm across his forehead. Summer had arrived in force. The sun had beat down on them all day. They still had another hour or so to go, but it had been a long, hard week. They all deserved a break. He signaled to Turner to let the crew go early for the day. The men gave him grateful looks as they retreated to their tents.

"Need help, Boss?" Big Jim asked, Turner right behind him, as Monroe searched the building for tools and supplies left behind.

"I've got it. Go on, get some rest."

The two left, and Monroe finished his scouting before retreating to his own tent. He should light a fire and make something to eat, but the weariness caught up with him and he opted to lie down instead.

It felt as if he'd only just laid down when he shot straight up in bed, his heart hammering. Peering through the darkness, his brain fumbled to figure out what had woken him.

All was quiet in the camp around him. His ears strained for the slightest noise over the sound of his own breathing. A horse nickered. An owl hooted, followed by the sound of the breeze rustling canvas tents and the call of a coyote.

His breathing slowed and, satisfied nothing was wrong, Monroe lay back down, arm over his eyes.

But sleep wouldn't come, and the old thoughts drifted into his mind.

Frustrated, he threw off the blankets and felt around for his boots. He hadn't even bothered to take his clothes off. Boots on, he found his hat lying on a stack of notes and blueprints.

Outside, the air had a slight chill to it at night, as it nearly always did in the various mountain valleys and canyons where he'd worked. The coldest had to have been the canyon northwest of Denver, where he'd constructed a railroad company's office for mere pennies. It was a beautiful place, though, filled with a raging river, songbirds, and steep mountains on either side of the canyon. He and Colette had been just over a year at that point, and that had been the third building job he'd taken on. She'd begged him not to, asked him to find work in Denver instead. But he'd insisted he needed the experience of building for a company, rather than another house or ranch building. So they'd gone, and while he gained experience and connections, Colette had retreated even further into herself the two months they were there.

Those were the thoughts that usually kept him up at night, that haunted his dreams even after he slept. Things he should've done, guilt over what he did, futile prayers to have that time back and make everything different. Only one thing seemed to drive them away—Emma.

Instinctively, Monroe glanced at the house down the hill and across the tracks. It was a moonless night, and not a single light was visible. No wonder—it had to be after midnight. His camp was completely dark too. Even the men who usually went to the mining encampment for a night's entertainment seemed to have chosen sleep instead. But he wasn't about to lie down and have those dreams dance across his mind again.

As a precaution, he threw on his guns, then reemerged from the tent and began to walk. Down the hill, and then right along the tracks, headed south. The breeze picked up again, sending the cold right through the shirt he wore. Had he thought this through, he would've grabbed his coat before leaving the tent. But the stars were bright in the sky overhead, and the coyote called again, creating a peace for which it was worth suffering a bit of chill.

He turned left, westward, along the worn path that led to the mining encampment and the mountains beyond that. To the left, a copse of trees hid a tiny stream that had already gone dry this summer. He had almost passed it when a faint cry came from somewhere behind the trees.

Monroe stopped short, his heart racing again. Perhaps it was an animal. Except it had sounded unmistakably human. Most likely, it was one of his crew who'd gone to the encampment, imbibed more than he could handle, and then gotten lost on the way back. Monroe sighed. Rescuing a drunk employee was not what he'd hoped for when setting off on this walk, but he could hardly leave the man to shiver outside all night. And it wasn't as if he'd had a destination in mind.

Stepping off the path, Monroe made his way through the long grass and the small bushes of sage and wildflowers he couldn't identify in the dark. When he reached the trees, he paused to listen.

Silence, and then the sound of twigs breaking. It came from straight ahead. Monroe maneuvered around the cottonwoods and pines until he heard a voice.

"Go away!"

Blood pumped faster through his veins. It was Emma, he was certain of it. What the devil she was doing this far from the house at this time of night was beyond him, but she sounded terrified. And she was speaking to someone.

As silently as possible, he stepped through the trees in front of him. He could just barely make out a small clearing where the stream usually ran down from the nearby foothills. And there—just to his left—was Emma. She had both arms outstretched in front of her, and she was looking straight ahead. He kept behind an evergreen and followed her line of vision to his right, a hand resting on the revolver in his belt.

Just beyond the dry creek bed, a hulking figure weaved to the left and then to the right.

A bear.

In the dark, he couldn't tell what kind of bear it was, but it was plenty obvious the thing was angry. It was up on its hind legs, grunting and growling.

"Emma." Monroe stepped out from behind the trees, his eyes on the bear. "Put your arms up over your head. Make yourself look as big as possible." He lifted his own arms as he moved toward her slowly.

If she was surprised to see him, she didn't show it. Instead, she did exactly as he said.

"Follow me." He made eye contact with the bear again and waved his arms. "Get out now, bear! Go on! Get!"

Emma followed suit, yelling at the bear in a voice that went from wavery to strong. They kept at it, holding their ground until the bear finally dropped to all fours, snuffled, and then ambled away into the trees.

Monroe lowered his arms when he was certain the bear had gone. He turned to Emma. "Are you all right?"

Emma was breathing hard, but she smiled when she looked at him. "I think so. How did you find me?"

"I heard your shout as I was walking by." He pulled off his hat and ran his arm across his forehead. Despite the cool night, he was drenched in sweat, and he wasn't certain he would ever catch his breath.

Fear.

He was outright scared to death over what could have happened to her. What was she doing out here anyway?

She watched him with doe eyes, dark hair escaping from the long braid that hung down her back, shawl slipping off the shoulders of her work dress. She smiled again. It was the middle of the night and she'd nearly been mauled by a bear, and she was smiling.

Monroe couldn't decide if he was angry or impressed. But one thing he knew for sure—he was terrified. "You can't do things like this."

Her forehead wrinkled. "Like what?"

"Walk out here in the dead of night. This isn't some fashionable district of town with a police officer on every corner ready to save you." It came out harsher than he'd intended, but maybe it would make her understand. He'd prefer to have her angry with him than dead.

She drew herself up taller and tugged the shawl together under her chin. "Mr. Hartley, I'm fairly certain I know where I am. And might I point out that you, too, are walking out here in the dead of night?"

"It isn't the same."

She lifted her eyebrows. "Oh? Right. I'm a woman. I'd forgotten."

It was a challenge. She wanted him to admit that was exactly the case. "Perhaps that's why. Have you forgotten what happened at the creek?"

"I have not. But that was during daylight hours. Should I stay shut up indoors at all times?"

"That's not what I meant."

She tilted her head and studied him. "Then what did you mean? Please, enlighten me."

This woman was so very different than Colette. His wife never would've been possessed by any force that made her want to stroll about the valley in the dark. The very thought would have terrified her. Of course, that was all his doing. If he hadn't dragged her away from everything she'd known to the most godforsaken places he could find, perhaps she would have remained that lively, happy girl he had married.

Colette also never would have challenged him like this. If she had, maybe she would still be alive.

Monroe choked back the guilt that tried to fight its way out from every part of him. Emma stood there, one hand on her hip, the other pinching her shawl together, waiting for his explanation. She was fire, this girl. And he needed an answer, fast. He cleared his throat. "You were almost a late supper for that bear. It was sheer luck that I happened to be nearby and heard you." He couldn't think about what might have happened if he had managed to sleep tonight. But at the same time, he couldn't push away the relief he felt. "I've lost too many people. I can't . . ." *I can't lose you, too.* But he couldn't say it. It wasn't fair to say that to her, not when whatever they might have was impossible.

Her face softened, and she let her hand drop from her shawl. "Your parents. And your sister." She took a hesitant step toward him. "Monroe, I'm sorry to have scared you so. I'm thankful you were here."

"I am too."

She reached a hand out to his arm and rested it on his wrist. It was a gesture meant to comfort. He closed his eyes briefly, and then took a step backward. Her hand fell away. "Emma," he started, and then stopped. He wasn't sure what to say. Neither of them could afford to put themselves into a situation that risked their positions here again. Then he almost chuckled. They were already in a dangerous place, alone together in the dead of night. They were already risking everything.

"I know," she said softly.

He could swear her eyes held the greatest sadness. She could've left by now. Simply said *thank you* and headed back to the house, as she should have. But she didn't. Instead, she was still here, seemingly as unwilling to leave as he, watching him with an expression that almost brought tears to his eyes.

"I was married." The words tumbled from his mouth without a second thought.

Emma said nothing. She raised her eyebrows and tilted her head a bit to the right, indicating she was waiting to hear more.

He swallowed hard. He'd told no one he'd met since Colette's death about her. Her passing was his terrible secret to keep, his burden to carry. He couldn't even try to puzzle out why he wanted to tell Emma now. But he did. For whatever crazy reason, he wanted her to know. "Her name was Colette. Her father owned the ranch where I worked after my father died. She became friendly with my sister first. But after about a year or so, I found myself talking with her here and there. After my sister disappeared . . . Colette was there. Every time I needed her, she was there. We fell in love, and we married."

Speaking about it made it feel as if it happened merely yesterday. Colette's warm smile, her uncanny ability to know whether he needed to laugh or simply be quiet for a while, her hand on his own, offering him comfort. She had given him all of that—everything she had—and all he could seem to do was stay selfishly focused on his own dreams.

"What happened to her?" Emma asked, her voice quiet.

Monroe took a deep breath. "We lived for a while on the ranch, hoping Lizzie would write or reappear, but I wanted to build. That meant leaving and moving from place to place." He paused. He couldn't do it. He couldn't put into words what he'd done. With that same old guilt eating him away from the inside out, all he could say was, "She died. In a mining camp a little ways southwest of Denver."

Emma's warm hand found his arm again. This time, he didn't step away. Instead, he closed his eyes and let her touch try to drive away the memories. He didn't deserve it—he didn't deserve her. When he opened his eyes again, Emma was but a heartbeat away. He reached out with his other hand and tucked the hair that had fallen from her braid behind her ear. Her small hand wrapped around his arm, and he let his hand linger on her neck. That lemon scent of her filled all of his senses. All he had to do was step forward. All he wanted to do was press her to him and keep her there forever.

He shouldn't. He *couldn't* if this work meant anything to him after all he'd given up for it. Yet somehow, it was impossible not to. It was almost as if a string tied them together and someone was pulling either end up, forcing him to move closer to Emma.

Eyes on hers, he took that one step. Barely any space separated them, and he could almost feel her breathing quicken. She raised a hand and placed it on his chest. Her eyes were almost gray in the dark as they held his. But then something flickered across them, driving away the curiosity and the desire that was there a split second ago.

Chapter Nineteen

Emma pressed her hand flat against Monroe's chest. Even as she pushed him away, she could feel his heart beat beneath her palm. Her own heart pounded like a drumbeat as her thoughts swirled and some deep part of her wanted nothing more than to let him pull her against him, consequences notwithstanding.

But there were consequences, and as powerful as the desire was to surrender every part of her being to this man, some still-functioning part of her brain screamed at the suffering it would cause her family.

"Monroe." The word was more breath than voice. She kept her hand on his chest and opened her eyes. "I can't. I'm sorry."

Sadness etched itself across his face as he laid a hand over hers. "I know."

"Mrs. Ruby spoke to me about what happened at the hotel. And then after that, I received a letter from home." She let her hand fall from his chest, but he kept his hand wrapped around hers. Her eyes pricked at the thought of what her family must be facing. She only hoped her first month's wages had reached them by now. "My sister Lily wrote and told me that she had to spend nearly all our remaining funds on Mama's doctor. I sent my wages, but I don't know if they arrived in time."

He held her hand tighter, but said nothing, letting her voice her fears out loud.

"What if I'm too late? They could have no place to live, and I'll have failed them." A sob choked its way up into her throat, and try as she might to push it back down, it consumed her.

Monroe drew her to him and wrapped his arms around her back. He held her for a moment until she could breathe again and the tears began to dry on her face. When his arms drifted gently from her, Emma took a step back, wiping at her eyes and wishing she could let him hold her forever.

"Even if that did happen," he said, "they would have received your wages soon after. And with that money, they can find a new place to live. So you have no reason to worry."

She gave him a small smile. He was right. "Thank you."

He returned her smile and her shoulders relaxed. What she would give to have him in her life, to allow him to court her openly, to . . . She drew in a breath. It was no use wishing for the impossible. Besides, he hadn't indicated he wished to court her anyway, which should be no surprise to her since he would lose this job he wanted so badly. And would she be willing to give up this new life she'd found? She couldn't picture Monroe stifling her in any way. Still . . .

"I . . ." She drifted off, uncertain how to phrase what needed to be said.

Monroe took both of her hands in his, and she almost lost all her resolve.

"I wish it were different," he said.

Her entire body warmed, reassured that he felt the same as she did. And thankful that she didn't have to tell him she could no longer see him. "As do I."

He looked down at her hands in his. Emma had felt nothing so safe, so comforting, so perfect in her life. *It's for my family*, she reminded herself before she pulled her hands from his. Her fingers instantly grew cold.

"I promise not to put your position here at risk," he said, his voice sounding a bit strangled. He cleared his throat. "May I walk you back?"

She nodded, not trusting herself to speak actual words for fear they'd be the ones she wanted more than anything to say.

He led the way back through the trees. Emma followed, fixing her eyes on his back. When she couldn't fall asleep earlier, this walk had seemed just the thing. In fact, her mind had been so tortured with fear for her family and confusion over what she felt for Monroe, the thought of facing Mrs. Ruby after breaking the rules seemed almost preferable. Just as she'd stepped into the hallway, Penny had awoken and offered to accompany her. Emma had turned her down, but accepted Penny's offer to make excuses to Mrs. Ruby if needed.

Now, as she came alongside Monroe into the open valley, Emma couldn't decide if this had been a good idea or not. Instead of feeling better, she was even more confused. Monroe had suffered a great loss and had confided in her. And it seemed as if he had feelings for her too, which filled her with a joy she couldn't even name—but then a terrible emptiness overshadowed anything good she felt. It was almost as if she were losing her father all over again. But how could she lose something she'd never even had?

Emma sighed, and Monroe turned to look at her. She smiled at him, as best she could, though it betrayed how she truly felt inside. He watched her, his mouth bereft of its usual lilt and his eyes empty of their normal light when he saw her.

She faced forward, searching out any sign of the buildings ahead, as the thoughts jumbled through her mind. One thing was absolutely clear—Monroe was just as confused as she was.

"SOMETHING'S BOTHERING you." Penny handed Emma a scoop of flour. It was early the next morning, and while Penny had been awake when Emma returned, Emma's thoughts had been so jumbled that all she could do was squeeze her eyes shut and pray for sleep.

"It's nothing." Emma added the flour to the mix and continued to stir.

Penny watched silently for a moment. Then she took a breath. Emma braced herself for more questions.

"I'm certain it's nothing. That's why you're about to overstir that batter and ruin our breakfast."

"Oh!" Emma glanced down. Sure enough, the batter was a little too smooth. Sighing, she passed the bowl to Penny. "Perhaps you should take over?"

Penny laughed. "This is the first time anyone has ever asked me to take over the cooking." She scooped out the batter and let it drip into little round cakes in the sizzling hot pan.

As the batter began to bubble around the edges, Emma wondered what kind of stove the new little apartment had, and whether Lily and Grace had mastered any of their family's favorite recipes yet. This, she decided, was far better than running her mind in circles with the fear that her family had no place to live, never mind a stove. Monroe was likely right about her money having arrived. She needed to believe that.

"Folks back home always said I was a good listener," Penny said. She flipped the first cake so it would cook evenly. Then she glanced at Emma. "I know I come off like a brash gossip, but I can keep the important things to myself. If you have important things you'd like to ease off your mind, that is."

Emma glanced about the kitchen. They were alone. Dora and Caroline had gone for more water, and Mrs. Ruby was in her office, settling correspondence. Meanwhile, Penny was here, watching Emma with a face so earnest, so ready to hear the secrets that make a friendship, it reminded Emma of Lily and of her friend Susannah at home, with whom she'd been close until the Daniels' decline in fortune had pulled them apart.

Perhaps it would ease her mind to speak the words aloud to a new friend. "It's . . . well, it's complicated."

Penny expertly flipped the cakes off the pan, as if she'd been doing this all her life instead of only six weeks. "In my experience, girls who look as you do right now are hung up on a beau."

Emma nearly choked on her own tongue.

"Of course," Penny said, glancing at her, "we Gilbert Girls don't have any beaux, do we?" The corner of her mouth turned up in just such a way that Emma knew for certain she could trust Penny with anything. Even the secret that could cost her everything.

"No, but . . ." Emma trailed off as she tried to figure out how to tell Penny about what existed between herself and Monroe.

"It's the fellow we met the first day, isn't it? The one who fixed your trunk?" Penny ladled in the last of the water to create more batter.

Emma's face warmed. "It is," she said carefully. "But it isn't as if anything—"

"What do you want?"

"I'm sorry?"

Penny stopped stirring and looked Emma square in the eyes. "If there was nothing standing between you two—if you were free for him to court you—what would you want to happen?"

Emma blinked at her. She hadn't let her thoughts get that far. She hadn't dared. Except . . . she had. Late at night, just before fully waking in the morning, bored while hanging laundry, her mind wandered. Images of a life with Monroe as her husband flickered behind her eyes, like photographs brought to life. The places they would see together as they moved from town to ranch to railroad depot—the freedom such a life would bring would make it feel as if she'd lost none of her newfound independence. Monroe, creating buildings from nothing as she tried to capture it all in poetry. Children dashing from a hastily put-together cabin to their father's latest half-finished project. Her mother and siblings perhaps moved somewhere nearby.

The realness—the utter, absolute happiness—of it all unnerved her so much that she had to grab on to the wooden countertop to keep from toppling over backward.

"I'd want it all," Emma said, her voice quiet.

Penny smiled knowingly at her. "Then there's your answer."

"But—"

Penny held up a finger. "No excuses. If you know what you want, you find a way to make it happen. Trust me, it's the best thing you can do for yourself."

Emma scrunched up her eyebrows, trying to read the meaning in between Penny's words. But the other girl seemed to have drifted off into her own thoughts. Emma moved across the room on shaky legs to retrieve the breakfast dishes.

What did she want? That was clear enough. But she also wanted security for her family. And that couldn't happen if she followed what was in her heart.

Could it?

Emma stood staring at the cabinet, the plain white dishes looking back at her.

If you know what you want, you find a way to make it happen.

Her contract with the Gilbert Company was only a year. If Monroe felt the same way about her, surely he would agree to wait for her. It would give him time to finish his work here, too, without fear of reprisal from Mr. Gilbert. The only problem that remained was how to care for her family if she no longer had this position. There had to be a way, even if she couldn't think of it right now. But perhaps if she told Monroe—if he knew that was the real reason she pulled away—he might be able to help her figure out what to do. Maybe he knew of work she could do as they moved. She wasn't too proud to take in laundry or do mending or cook meals. If anything, being a Gilbert Girl had taught her that she was capable of nearly any task put to her.

Her entire demeanor lifted with hope, so much that Mrs. Ruby had to ask her twice during breakfast if she remembered how to best appease a guest who disliked the dish he ordered. Penny gave her a smile, and Emma didn't even mind having to ask Mrs. Ruby to repeat herself.

After they'd finished breakfast and hung the laundry, Dora and Caroline took charge of cooking the noon meal, Penny went for tutoring with Mrs. Ruby on what she called "conversation starters," and Emma found herself with a dilemma. She had one hour until she'd be needed to serve the meal. Mrs. Ruby expected the girls to use these short breaks to review the dining protocols they'd be using in the hotel or to catch up on unfinished tasks. Emma's best dress was in sore need of ironing, and it wouldn't hurt her to review, but the door to the house seemed to pull her outside, toward Monroe.

If she could just speak with him for a few minutes and tell him what she'd realized that morning, maybe he could be of help. If he knew that was the only thing holding her back, perhaps . . .

Emma's smile nearly touched her ears as she moved quickly across the sage and grasses. Summer in this valley was the most beautiful scene she had ever laid eyes on. Some of the snow had melted off the mountains to the west, but a lot of it still remained. The peaks set a stunning backdrop to the greens and yellows of the valley. Large white clouds moved lazily across the sky, and a bee buzzed past Emma's nose. She swatted it away absentmindedly as she kept her eyes on the structure straight ahead. Once over the tracks, she climbed the hill until the hotel lay spread out before her.

There was still much to be done inside, but it was hard to know that from the outside. Soaring windows, lofty eaves, and wide, welcoming doors made this a place weary travelers would be glad to visit. Emma could almost hear the planned fountain gurgling out front as she stood still and admired the place that Monroe had created. It was but a skeleton when she'd arrived, and now it was an almost-whole building.

She felt so proud of him that she wanted to run and find every person in this valley and show off what Monroe had made out of nothing at all.

"Miss Daniels, do you need some help?" A tall man, red-faced from the sun with dark blond hair slicked under his hat, had emerged from around the corner of the building.

"No, sir. I'm simply admiring your work." Emma smiled out of habit, but then drew it back when she realized he'd said her name. "I'm sorry, do I know you?"

He pulled off his hat and ran a hand over his hair to smooth it. "I'm afraid not, but I remember you from the investors' tour." He paused for a moment, almost as if he expected her to apologize. Although for what, she had no idea. "I'm John Turner, the foreman."

Emma pushed her lips together, searching for any memory of the man. When she came up short, she gave him her kindest smile and said, "I'm so sorry, I don't remember you being there."

"I wasn't," he said shortly. Then he softened. "But I saw you and the other ladies from a distance. I don't forget true beauty when it crosses my path."

It was a compliment, and Emma nodded to accept it, although there was something about the way he said it—or maybe it was the way he looked at her—that made gooseflesh rise on her skin.

Mr. Turner took a step back. "I apologize. I'll let you go on your way."

Emma swallowed. She was being silly. Monroe's foreman wouldn't harm her. She was simply shaky from her experience down at the creek weeks ago. "It was nice to meet you, Mr. Turner." With that, she moved on shaky feet across the sandy dirt and flattened grasses toward the corner of the hotel. When she looked back, Mr. Turner had disappeared around the other corner.

Emma paused to catch her breath. From here, just a few feet away from the open windows—and they were real glass windows!—of the hotel, the echoes of voices and hammers created quite a din from inside. Emma moved slowly around the building, taking in everything that had changed since she'd last been here. Around the back, she spotted the one person she'd hoped to see. He was alone, scratching out something with a pencil on a scrap of paper. She stood there for a moment, simply watching him. That was safe. No one who happened upon them could suspect anything with them at this much of a distance from each other.

He scrunched up his face and his lips moved as he wrote while standing. At one point, he pushed his hat back a little and scratched at his forehead. He was in his usual work clothes—dark gray pants, a white shirt, a black vest, and the same scuffed boots. He looked so handsome, just standing there, figuring up whatever it was he was working on, that Emma had to remind herself to breathe.

He paused, and she wondered if it was because he knew she was there. When he looked up, a wide, lazy smile crossed his face. Then it was almost as if he remembered what they'd last discussed. The smile disappeared, and he scanned the area before letting his eyes come to rest on her again.

"I need to speak with you," she said.

Monroe's eyebrows rose, and that devil-may-care smile slowly returned. He folded the paper he'd been writing on into a neat little square and slid it into his pocket before gesturing toward the nearest door to the hotel, which was propped open.

Emma hesitated a moment. Wasn't his crew inside the hotel? It wouldn't do to have anyone happen upon them. No—she needed to trust him. He wouldn't take her anywhere someone could find them, after all. He was much too careful for that.

She scurried forward and slipped through the door. He was waiting for her just inside. She shut the door firmly behind her and glanced down the hallway.

"No one is down here," he said. "We're working upstairs today."

Relief flooded her chest. As she looked up at him in the dim light, she wondered how she managed to find someone so right for her all the way out here in the wilderness of Colorado. It was almost as if she came here because of some divine intervention.

Monroe stood a foot away, hands in his pockets, every inch the gentleman. "Emma?" he prompted. "Is everything all right?"

She twisted her hands together, and she could almost hear her mother scolding her for fidgeting. She pulled them apart and looked up into his eyes. Eyes she could drown in. Which wouldn't help her at all, considering what she needed to ask him.

Asking him. She'd been so caught up in the idea of Monroe having the answer, and so excited about the possibilities that might create, she hadn't really thought through *how* she would ask him. *I'll marry you if you know of some way I can earn money while we travel from place to place* didn't quite seem the right way, considering he hadn't proposed.

He stood there patiently, watching her search for the right words. "Was there something you wanted to ask me?"

Emma nodded. "I . . . if . . ." Why hadn't she thought this through?

Monroe's lips quirked up into that smile—the one that was teasing, the one that put her almost beside herself that first day she'd met him. "Do you need help with your poetry again? I can't say I'm any sort of poet, but how about *His eyes were like dewfall on the dirt / white and brown just like his shirt*?"

Emma almost snorted with laughter. "And why do you think I'm writing poetry about you?"

"I didn't say those exquisite lines were about me." He raised his eyebrows. "*Are* you writing poetry about me? Because I'd be quite honored."

Her cheeks went warm. He lifted a hand and rested his fingers gently on her cheek. She closed her eyes. It was as if his hand and her face were the only things that existed in the world. His thumb caressed her jawbone, and a sigh escaped her throat.

"The way you smile . . ." He ran his thumb over her lips, and she thought she might melt from his touch. "It reminds me . . . I never thought such a memory could be anything but tainted, but you've proven otherwise."

She opened her eyes, expecting to see a tinge of sadness on his face. But there was none. Instead, he smiled slightly, and his eyes were even darker than usual. She needed to ask him—to find out if any of this was possible. The right words didn't matter, only the answer he might have. "Monroe." Her voice came out strangled with emotion.

"I know." His hand lifted just a fraction from her face, but she caught it with her own, pressing it back against her cheek and resting her palm on the back of his hand.

"I was wondering—"

A thump and the sound of the door flying open took the words from her mouth.

Chapter Twenty

"Boss?" John Turner stood there in the doorway, a dark figure outlined by the bright sun. His eyes went directly to Monroe's hand on Emma's face, just a split second before Monroe dropped it.

Monroe backed away, for all the good it did. It was too late, and all he could hope was that Turner was not the sort of man to turn tail and tell McFarland or Mrs. Ruby. Especially after all that Monroe had done for him. "What do you need?" The words came out short, and Monroe inwardly wished he could take them back.

"Well . . ." The man drew the word out as he leaned against the doorframe. A smile played across his lips as his eyes roved over Emma. He removed his hat and held it lazily against his thigh. "Miss."

Monroe stepped in front of her, blocking her from Turner's perusal. His heart thumped out a warning. Something felt very wrong. "Did your men finish the molding?"

Turner nodded. "We did. I came to let you know Daley's crew is finished with the south side, but now something else has my attention."

Monroe's fingers tapped out a rhythm on his legs. "Something with which you don't need to concern yourself."

Turner smiled even wider as he crossed his arms. "See, Boss, it is, though. If you're off cavorting with one of them Gilbert Girls, how are we supposed to finish this work on time?"

Bile rose in Monroe's throat as heat flooded his entire body. Behind him, Emma placed a hand on his back, almost as if she could tell he was teetering on the edge. He'd been a fool, convincing himself to trust this man. What he really wanted to do was punch Turner in his grinning face, but instead, he concentrated on Emma's hand and said, "Are you going to run off and tell McFarland? Ruin everything we've worked for?"

Turner shrugged. "It don't much matter to me who I'm working for, so long as I get the money promised when we beat that deadline. It's you—and her—whose positions are at stake. But I could remain quiet." He left the word hanging.

Monroe grunted. He didn't trust himself with words, and he had more than an inkling about what was coming next.

"I could be persuaded."

"You could." Monroe's voice was flat. "Dare I ask how?"

"You know, we don't make much in the way of coin here." Turner paused and ran a hand over the fine woodwork on the doorframe as if he actually cared about the work. "A body tends to run out near the end of the week and has to forgo spirits and all manner of entertainments over at the mining camp. Pardon me, miss." He ducked his head toward Emma.

She stilled behind Monroe, but kept her hand on his back. That wave of heat rose through him again. He'd see Turner run out of camp before he could do anything that would hurt Emma. "And?" he said, fire igniting the word.

"And a little more in the way of pocket money might go far in keeping my mouth shut."

Turner was blunt, Monroe gave him that. He stared the man down for a moment as he fought to control the inferno that threatened to overflow. "How much?"

"Oh, I don't know. How about you make me an offer?" Turner stood up straight, one hand in his pocket and the other replacing his hat.

Monroe dug his teeth into the insides of his lips. The last thing he wanted to do was give this waste of a man his own hard-earned money. But if it protected Emma and kept him here to finish his work and get the reference he so badly needed, he'd do just about anything. He held out a couple of bills.

Turner's eyes widened. "That'll do just nicely, I think." He pocketed it. "You know this'll be gone by Friday next?"

"Right." Monroe growled out the word.

"I believe I'll tell Daley to take his men to work on the north wing." Turner doffed his hat to Emma and disappeared past them into the hallway that led to the front entrance and the grand staircase.

Monroe was quiet for a moment before stepping forward to shut the open door. He could barely comprehend what had just happened. The man he'd seen a little of himself in had just weaseled his way into taking Monroe's money to keep quiet. Turner was nothing like him, nothing at all. He should've trusted his instincts, especially after Turner had shown who he truly was in front of the investors. But instead, Monroe had forced himself to interpret Turner's impatience and constant peacocking for attention as the same ambition Monroe had felt when he'd first started building.

It wasn't even remotely the same. That he could see, now that it had smacked him in the face.

"He's blackmailed you." Emma looked up at him, her eyes filled with a fire that matched his own.

"I know," Monroe said shortly, then immediately hated himself for taking his frustration out on her. "I'm sorry. I'm angry—with him, and with myself for giving in to him."

"What are you going to do?" Emma asked. She clutched her arms to her stomach, and he wondered if it was from fear or anger.

"I don't know." He ran a hand through his hair. "I don't see that we have any other options, though. I need to finish this project and secure a reference, and you need to keep your position and your reputation."

Emma pushed her lips together, and he softened.

He reached for her hand. "I apologize for putting you into this situation. For not remaining true to what I promised." His eyes drifted from her face to her hand in his. He shouldn't be holding it. He shouldn't have touched her at all. He should have sent her away the second she stepped foot behind the hotel.

"It isn't your fault." She gave him a sad smile. "I came here of my own free will."

Monroe found her eyes again. He could lose his very soul in those eyes. "I promise not to put you in such a position ever again. You deserve better." *You deserve a man who will give you the life you want, who won't force you to move from town to ranch to mining camp, who will make you happy.* He gently pulled his hand from hers.

Her throat bobbed as she swallowed, but she didn't say a word.

"You wanted to ask me a question, I believe?"

Emma pushed her lips together again. She had a habit of doing that, and he hadn't quite figured out what it meant. He wanted to learn, though. He wanted to know everything there was to know about this woman. Perhaps after their work here was finished . . . No, it was foolish to even entertain such a thought. Selfish. He'd always been selfish, and it had cost the life of one woman he'd loved already.

He couldn't do that to Emma.

"I've forgotten it," Emma said, her voice as soft as a silk pillow he'd once laid his head on. That had been at a hotel in Denver, where he'd spent every penny he had trying to kill the grief and the guilt after Colette's death.

Monroe waited, but Emma offered nothing else. She wrapped her arms around herself, and with that one simple move, he'd never felt further apart from her.

"I should go." She'd already taken a step toward the door. Away from him.

A great, gaping canyon opened in Monroe's heart. "Emma."

She paused, eyes on him but still so far away.

"Maybe . . ." he said, but his voice was full of pebbles. He cleared his throat and with it, his sense. He couldn't give her the hope of something that couldn't happen. "I'll make certain Turner stays quiet."

She gave him a brief smile, her eyes more watery than normal. When she disappeared out the door, she took a piece of him with her.

Chapter Twenty-one

Tuesday morning dawned with a bright sky and clouds on the horizon. As Emma waited out front with Mrs. Ruby, Mrs. McFarland, and the other girls, she felt that the sky accurately represented her soul. She had a bright future with the Gilbert Company, but no amount of praise from Mrs. Ruby or promise of money for her family could replace the clouds and emptiness she felt inside. They waited patiently for the train to arrive from Denver and Cañon City, carrying four new girls that Emma and the others would be expected to teach everything about the Gilbert Company way. More girls would arrive slowly over the next few weeks.

Penny could barely conceal her excitement at meeting some new faces, and even Caroline was fidgeting. Dora, however, looked as if she had something else on her mind. Emma empathized, because she did too, and it wasn't just the loneliness she'd felt since she'd last parted from Monroe a few days ago. This train would likely carry a letter from home, and while she was eager for news, every terrible event that might have befallen her family had run through her mind. She prayed every night and every morning that her wages had been reaching them on time. And though she'd written to her sisters and her mother multiple times, she'd only received the one return letter so far.

The sound of hammers and shouts drew her attention away from the tracks on the horizon. The men had begun their day's work on the hotel. She sighed as she watched them work on some large wooden piece lying in front of the hotel while the grand doors opened wide to show the inside of the lobby. From this distance, it wasn't possible to tell who was who, and that was for the best.

After what had happened a few days ago with Mr. Turner, she vowed to herself that she would not seek Monroe out again. Not only because of the danger to both of them, but because that moment had made it crystal clear that anything between them simply wasn't possible. What was it he'd said, just as she'd gathered up the courage to ask him the question she'd intended to voice before Turner interrupted them? *I promise not to put you in such a position ever again. You deserve better.*

With those words, she'd swallowed the one hope she had that something could work out between them. It was for the best, she'd told herself. Finding respectable work as a married woman was nigh impossible enough, and finding it when one didn't live in a fixed place was even harder. She couldn't expect Monroe to solve that problem for her. It was foolish to have even entertained the thought. Her first duty was to her family, and she'd do well to remember that. Monroe would finish his work here within the next month or two, and then he would move on while she served out the remainder of her contract. If the company would have her, she'd sign on for another year. Followed by another and another. And to that end, she would remain unmarried, possibly forever.

"You look so sad," Dora whispered.

Emma nearly jumped. Dora rarely confided in her, and she had never asked Emma about anything personal. Penny had asked, of course, earlier that morning, but Emma's sorrowful look had given her all the answers she'd needed.

"I am, a little," Emma finally whispered back. "But I will be fine."

Dora gave her a tentative smile. But her eyes, so dark they were almost black, looked a million miles away.

"You are too, I can tell," Emma said.

They said nothing else, but simply stood there in mutual understanding until a whistle pierced the air and steam filled the horizon to the north.

"They're coming!" Penny said.

Mrs. Ruby laid a hand on her arm to still her.

"Pardon," Penny said, but she still stood on her tiptoes as she looked north, like a small child eager for her father's return.

Emma's thoughts wandered back to Monroe as they waited for the train to arrive. If things were different, would he have asked for her hand? She wanted to hope he would have, that perhaps he planned to do so still, once his work here was finished. He knew about her family's situation, but she doubted he understood that their welfare would be her responsibility for years, until her brother was old enough to provide for them.

When she came out here, she was certain that this work and the freedom that came with it were all that she could ever want. But now she yearned for more. She wanted Monroe. She wanted to share a life with him, build a family with him. And the thought of staying on here after he left, alone and without him, sounded like a dismal future.

When the train screeched to its stop in front of them, Penny, Dora, and Caroline crowded around the door to the only car. When it opened, the four new girls who stepped out found themselves greeted enthusiastically.

Mrs. Ruby completed the introductions, and the new girls—Sarah, Jane, Beatrice, and Millie—seemed everything from excited to terrified. Emma hid a smile behind her hand. They reminded her so much of when she and the other girls had first arrived just six weeks ago. How much had changed since then! The new hotel actually looked like a hotel, and they'd all proven themselves to be much stronger than they'd ever thought.

As for Emma, her heart had changed in ways she'd never anticipated. She sighed and tried to push those thoughts aside as she followed the group back to the house.

Mrs. Ruby slowed to wait for her. "There is no letter, Emma. I'm sorry."

"Thank you." The words hid the worsening ache in her soul. She'd lost Monroe, and all she wanted right now were comforting words from home.

Mrs. Ruby laid a hand on Emma's arm. "You can ask after one when you next go into Cañon City for services."

Emma forced a smile she didn't feel.

After a late breakfast, and after the new girls were shown the bedroom they would need to share, Mrs. Ruby assigned Emma to take Millie to fetch water and begin washing the bed linens and towels. Together they set out toward the tracks and up the slope.

"Are you happy to be here?" Emma asked by way of making polite conversation. Millie hadn't said much at breakfast, and all Emma and the other girls had learned was that she was from St. Louis.

Millie shrugged. "It wasn't my choice, but I suppose there were worse options."

"Well, it really isn't so bad. It's hard work, but Mrs. Ruby is fair and patient. We attend services in Cañon City on Sundays. You can bring your earnings to send home then too, if you choose." She shifted the empty bucket from one hand to the other.

Millie said nothing, and Emma wondered if she didn't get along with her family. Perhaps her leaving had something to do with that, which could explain why she was so hesitant to speak on it. She seemed slightly older than Emma, maybe twenty-one or twenty-two. But Emma couldn't be sure if she actually was older, or if she simply exuded an air of greater maturity. Her bright red hair was swept up off her neck, and even the soft gray of the Gilbert Girl dress couldn't dull its lively effect.

"May we see the new hotel?" Millie asked.

Emma shifted her bucket to her other hand. She couldn't refuse, and she couldn't decide if she hoped to see Monroe or if she prayed he was elsewhere. She detoured closer to the building, and Millie's eyes lit up as she took in what was before her.

"It's magnificent," she said, almost breathless.

"It truly is a marvel. You should see the inside. Mrs. McFarland says it should be ready in less than a month," Emma said. A rush of pride flooded her as she took in the majestic building.

"Sooner, if I have any say in it," Monroe said from where he stepped out of the front doors. He doffed his hat. "Ladies."

Emma's throat went dry at the mere sight of him. Would he ever stop having that effect on her? Especially now that all hope they had to be together was gone.

Millie dipped her head and looked at Monroe through her lashes. Something about the look set Emma on edge. Her hand tightened around the rope handle of the water bucket, and she gritted her teeth. Only after a few seconds passed did she remember she should make introductions. "Miss Sinclair, this is Mr. Monroe Hartley. Mr. Hartley is the hotel's builder. Miss Sinclair is one of the new Gilbert Girls."

To his credit, Monroe merely nodded at Millie and said the standard reply about how glad he was to make her acquaintance. Then his eyes went right back to Emma. She warmed all over, reassured and feeling silly for being jealous.

Her mind whirled. *I promise not to put you in such a position ever again. You deserve better.* Emma had thought he had meant everything was over between them. But if that was true, why had he emerged from the hotel? Was it because she had Millie in tow? Even still, that didn't necessitate his coming outside.

He'd come to see her.

If there had been a fence post or a wall nearby, Emma would have grabbed on to it. Instead, all she could do was root her heels into the ground and pray not to topple over as the realization washed through her: Monroe still saw some flicker of hope for them. How, she had no idea. Perhaps it was as she'd thought a hundred times since she'd last parted from him—he had no idea how long her responsibility to her family would last. Maybe the words he had spoken meant only that he would never compromise her reputation again by spending time with her alone. And when his work here was finished . . .

She wanted to grab him by his arms and demand answers.

"What have we here? Visitors?"

The sound of that voice behind Monroe immediately stopped the thoughts racing through Emma's head. Monroe visibly tensed as John Turner joined their group.

"Miss Daniels. How nice to see you again." His smile bordered on lecherous, and Emma wanted nothing more than to smack his leering face. But instead, she took her anger out on the bucket handle, causing the rope to dig into her palm, and made introductions again.

Mr. Turner immediately turned all of his attention to Millie. "Meeting you, dear lady, is perhaps the best thing that has happened to me since I came to these parts."

Millie flushed a furious red, and Emma looped her arm protectively through the other girl's. Millie hadn't yet heard Mrs. Ruby's lecture, and she clearly couldn't see Turner for the louse that he was. Emma fixed Mr. Turner with a glare. "If you'll pardon us, Miss Sinclair and I need to fetch water for the wash."

Turner tipped his hat, and the grin he gave Millie made Emma's stomach turn. She glanced at Monroe, whose fists were balled at his sides. As she and Millie walked away, she breathed a sigh of relief. Monroe would set Turner right. Emma only hoped he didn't have to pay more for the privilege. The thought of Monroe giving any money to that no-good, conniving—

"He certainly was interesting, John." Millie's eyes were alight as they walked down toward the creek, and the fondness with which she said the man's name made Emma's jaw clench.

"*Mr. Turner* is not someone you want to know any better." Emma dropped Millie's arm to move the bucket to her other hand.

Millie picked her way around a large clump of sagebrush. "He was awfully charming. And . . ."

"And what?"

"He seemed to take to me. No man ever took to me at home." The flush crept up into her cheeks again.

Emma sighed. She knew exactly what Millie meant. "He's not worth losing your position here. Mr. Turner is not as he seems."

Millie scrunched up her face as she looked at Emma. "What do you mean?"

"I can't go into details. Please just trust me, Millie."

Millie said nothing else as they traversed the wagon-wide path to the creek. They filled the buckets in silence. On the way back, Emma took them the long way, giving the new hotel a wide berth—both for Millie's sake and her own. She couldn't allow herself to think more about Monroe's words and actions today until she was alone. When she glanced at Millie, the girl looked lost in thought, a little smile playing across her face.

The sight made Emma's insides twist up. She sent up a quick prayer that Millie would come to her senses, fast.

Chapter Twenty-two

Leaning against the rough plank wall, Monroe reread the handwritten telegram that McFarland had brought back that evening.

First guests to arrive third of August. Furnishings &c on twenty-fourth of July. If complete, new offer awaits. J.G. Gilbert, Jr.

The message was cryptic. Monroe refolded the paper and placed it carefully into his pocket. It seemed as if Gilbert was pleased enough with his progress so far that he wanted to offer him new work—but only if the hotel was ready for furnishings in a week and guests soon afterward.

There had been similar telegrams for Mrs. Ruby and the McFarlands, no doubt alerting them to the hotel's opening. Monroe wondered how Emma felt. Was she excited to begin working with the guests? To move into the real hotel? She'd been in his thoughts constantly, so much that he couldn't resist seeing her when she came to the hotel with the new Gilbert Girl. Just seeing her again made all the possibilities in the world run through his mind. Impossible possibilities.

He should go back inside. Big Jim had dealt him out of a hand of poker. It should be finished by now. Still, Monroe made no move to reenter the rickety building. Outside wasn't particularly peaceful, but it was better than the cramped space indoors. When he'd showed Big Jim the telegram, the larger man had clapped him on the back and offered to help him celebrate. He couldn't say no, even though he rarely went to the mining camp.

He wondered what Emma would think of the telegram. She'd be happy for him, he was certain of that. But he could almost see a shadow behind the joy that would light up her pretty green eyes. Because she couldn't go with him. A builder's life—constantly on the move, never staying in one place more than a few months—wasn't for a woman such as Emma. She needed a stable home. Some place she could fix up and raise children. He'd learned that the hard way.

Here he was, on the verge of having everything he'd wanted, and now . . .

A woman's shrill laugh cut through his thoughts. It was an odd sound, almost jarring, in this camp. There were no women here, save for the handful of whores who came and went when the company bosses moved them along because they distracted the men too much from their work. They were gone now, a fact made obvious the second he'd walked into the makeshift gambling house. They usually bided their time for at least a week somewhere up in the mountains before venturing back into the camp again.

The laugh came again, and it made Monroe finally move from his place holding up the wall. He peered down the trampled and packed dirt that acted as a street, bordered by the occasional hastily constructed building and even more dirty white tents. A few miners, many staggering under the weight of drink, made their way back and forth, and music poured out of one of the tents, but there was no sign of any woman. The laugh sounded again, but this time from behind him.

Monroe turned, and there, between the wall of the gambling house and the fluttering canvas that served as the wall of the bathhouse, he spotted her. It was too dark to make out any identifying features, but two figures—one of whom was clearly a woman—stood on the narrow strip of dirt.

He took a few steps forward, the canvas concealing him, until he could make out their voices.

"I swear, I ain't ever seen hair as pretty as yours." *Turner.*

Monroe's limbs turned to ice just hearing the man's voice. He was the reason Monroe's pocket was lighter than it should be, but worse than that—and worse than the fact that Monroe had ever seen a part of himself in that snake—he'd threatened Emma. It had taken every ounce of his willpower not to pummel the man when he joined them and the new girl by the hotel two days ago. Seeing him prey on this young girl only reinforced that urge.

She giggled. Turner placed his hands on her waist, and that was all Monroe could handle. He stepped out from behind the canvas and made his way toward the pair. Squinting through the darkness, he tried to make out the girl's features. Whore or not, all he wanted was to get her away from this sad excuse for a man. But she wasn't a whore. That much became clear the closer he got. Cherry-red hair, tall and thin . . . she was the new Gilbert Girl who'd been with Emma at the hotel.

That familiar fire tore through his veins. "That's enough."

Turner looked up at him. "Pardon? The lady and I were having a private conversation." Monroe couldn't make out his expression, but from the seething irritation in his tone, he didn't particularly need to.

Monroe held out a hand to the girl. "The lady needs to return to Crest Stone."

She glanced between them, Turner's hands still on her waist and her hat askew.

"Millie?" Turner asked the question of the girl but kept his eyes on Monroe. "Do you wish to be escorted home?"

"I . . . I came here to spend the evening with you." Miss Sinclair pulled an arm from under Turner's grasp and righted her hat.

Turner said nothing, but the smile on his face was enough to make Monroe want to knock it right off.

"Are you certain?" he asked Miss Sinclair, the growl in his voice just barely keeping his anger in check.

She tilted her head up to see him. "I am, sir. I do appreciate your riding to my rescue, though. You're quite gallant, Mr. Hartley."

"I know this won't be something that gets around camp, will it, Hartley?" Turner's eyes bored into him, but Monroe held his gaze.

"It will not." He ground the words out. Getting Turner dismissed was an excellent idea—but not at the cost of Emma's reputation and his own work.

With that, Turner pulled Miss Sinclair closer, and it was as if Monroe was no longer there.

Monroe clenched his fists and strode away from the couple. If the girl wanted to risk her own reputation and her employment, so be it. He'd done all he could. He passed the entrance to the gambling house and found Pender tied to a wooden post. He worked the knot apart. Big Jim would figure out that he'd returned to camp. Pender nipped at his hat.

"Not tonight, boy," he said, although Pender's big brown eyes and silly horse grin made Monroe smile. He rode past drunken miners and tents that had seen much better days until he was out in the valley. The mining camp sat at the base of the mountains, and it was a good two or three miles from the hotel.

Out on the valley floor, it was just him, the horse, and the stars. The cool air calmed the rage Turner seemed to bring on by his mere presence. Monroe breathed it in. The fresh breeze was like a balm to his soul. The air and the mountains and the wide open space of the valley were everything he needed. Even though he'd grown up in Kansas City and then in the chaos of a young Denver, this land spoke to him. It was as if he belonged here, out in the frontier where few white people had trod.

He'd first felt this way on Colette's parents' ranch. Something about the wilderness that surrounded it, the horses and cattle, the occasional visits from the few remaining Plains tribes, the room to simply exist without so many people crowding into his thoughts—it made living easier. It was where he had healed after the loss of both of his parents, where he'd fallen in love with Colette, where he'd tried in vain to keep his sister, and where he'd felt at home until he left with his wife. Since then, he'd stayed periodically in Denver and in smaller towns as he was hired for building jobs, but his favorite work was in places such as this.

Somewhere in the distance, a coyote yelped. The stars blinked overhead, and the crinkling in his pocket reminded him of what might lie ahead in his future. He pulled the telegram out again and clutched it in his hand. He could get the work done, he was certain. Even if he and the men had to go without sleep, they'd finish it. They'd earn the bonus, and now it seemed as if Mr. Gilbert had a new project for him. This was the biggest job of his life, and he'd almost done it. He'd almost proven himself a trustworthy and reputable builder, from nearly nothing at all. After this, doors would open for him anywhere he wanted to go. It was everything he'd ever wanted.

Almost everything.

He pushed the telegram back into his pocket and tilted his hat back. He never could have imagined Emma. But she was here, and she had worked her way into his very soul. He wished he could ask her to come with him, to marry him.

But he knew it wouldn't work. It hadn't for Colette, after all. His once vivacious, happy wife had turned quiet and pale and withdrawn. It was the height of selfishness to ask Emma to conform to this life he wanted for himself. That was even if she said yes. It could cost her life, and he wouldn't do that to her. But the thought of leaving her behind tore a hole in his heart that he feared would never heal.

The wind lifted the hair on the back of his neck. *Emma is different.*

He stared out into the darkness, unsure from where the thought had come. Emma was different than Colette, in many ways, even in the simple fact that she had chosen to leave behind everything she'd known to come out here to the godforsaken frontier, all alone. But that didn't make her any less likely to want the things most women wanted.

Did it?

Pender nickered, almost as if he knew Monroe's thoughts were getting more tangled the closer they got to home. Monroe leaned forward and rubbed the horse on his neck.

"What should I do?" he whispered.

The horse didn't answer, of course. But he knew he needed to speak with Emma. And he knew there was really no choice to be made. There never was. She deserved to know that he'd be moving on after his work here was finished in just a few weeks. It was too late tonight, but he'd find her first thing tomorrow morning, before work began for the day.

Idly, he imagined her throwing herself at him, begging him to take her with him. It wouldn't happen—she was much too well-bred to do such a thing. And that was for the best.

He cared far too much for Emma to see her waste away like Colette.

She deserved a better life than the one he could give her.

Chapter Twenty-three

The pre-dawn chill made Emma shiver as she walked down the back steps of the house. She yawned and waited for her eyes to adjust to the shadowy yard. Birds sang, but otherwise it was silent. Emma breathed deeply and a smile crossed her face. Never had she thought she would come to love early mornings. Back home, she and Lily would put off waking for as long as possible, much preferring to stay tucked into the warmth of their beds. But here . . . Something about the solitude and the majesty outdoors spoke to her. Just knowing all of what waited for her outside made her awaken before everyone else. Most of the poetry she'd written since she'd been here had been composed in the gray light of the early morning.

Her shoes sank into the sandy ground as she crossed the yard. One bird sang louder than the others. Halfway to the privy, she stilled. That was no bird. Clutching her shawl closer around her, Emma turned slowly, searching for the source of the sound. Around the barn, a figure emerged. The wild beating of her heart calmed—just a little—as she made out Monroe's features. She glanced quickly around her. No one else had stirred when she'd left the house, but she couldn't be certain that was still true.

Moving swiftly, she paced the rest of the distance to the barn. She followed Monroe around to the far side, which faced nothing but the empty valley and the dark Wet Mountains to the east.

He looked so handsome this morning, even with his vest a bit rumpled and his hair grown too long. Emma tilted her head back to see his face. She wanted more than anything to reach up and trace his firm jaw with her fingertips, but the fear of being discovered—and the fear that she'd misinterpreted his actions a few days ago—kept her hands at her sides. "The house will be awake any moment now." The second the words were out of her mouth, she wished she could take them back. It sounded as if she didn't want to see him at all, when the opposite was the truth. She wanted to see him, to talk to him, to find out his true feelings.

"I know. I'll be quick." He gazed at her with a look so protective it sent a wave of warmth through her body. "Would you be free to meet me at the creek? I have some news."

"Oh?" Emma's mind raced, trying to figure out what it might be. It had to be something good, given the enthusiasm with which he spoke. "I suppose I could offer to retrieve the water for washing. And the butter for breakfast." She said this as if weren't something she already did each day.

A smile creased Monroe's face, and it turned Emma into jelly. "There is an old footbridge that's fallen into disrepair a little ways south of the springhouse. Meet me there?"

Emma nodded just as the door to the house creaked open. The sound nearly made her jump. She turned reflexively, but of course, there was nothing to see on this side of the barn but the shadows of the mountains and the expanse of valley that led to them. "I must go."

"I'll wait for you by the creek." He paused a second and looked at her like a starving man. Then he leaned forward, and his lips grazed her cheek. "Go."

Emma turned and stepped around the side of the barn, barely giving herself time to become composed. Thank goodness the sun had only just begun to peek over the horizon. Otherwise, whoever had stepped into the yard would likely remark upon the shade of her cheeks.

Millie stood a few yards away, near the privy.

"Good morning!" Emma called, her voice a bit too cheerful.

Millie smiled at her. "Are you always awake before the sun?"

"Most days," Emma confessed, just as the door to the house opened and another of the new girls, Beatrice, stepped out. "I'll go to the springhouse, if you both would like to start frying the ham and the eggs." The eggs had been a pleasant surprise from Mrs. McFarland, who kept chickens.

"Do you need help with the water?" Millie asked.

Emma shook her head. "Thank you, but I'll be fine. I'm looking forward to that ham." That, at least, was not a lie. Once they moved into the hotel, they would begin keeping pigs and cows for meat and milk, in addition to the chickens Mrs. McFarland kept now. But for the present, Mr. McFarland brought slabs of ham back from town on occasion, and of course they had venison from the numerous mule deer in the area and beef from the ranchers in the valley.

"If you're certain?" Millie hesitated on the steps to the house, Beatrice having already slipped inside.

"I am." Emma gave her a warm smile. "In fact, I'm looking forward to the walk."

Beatrice returned and handed her a bucket, and after finally using the privy, Emma headed out. She forced herself to walk normally. After all, she had to give Monroe time to make it back. She looked around for him, but couldn't spot anyone beyond the men who milled around the campfires and tents on top of the rise. He must have left quickly after they parted, while the girls' attention was on her.

Emma chose a route that took her around the new hotel, opposite the side with the camp. It seemed smart to avoid seeing anyone right now, although there was certainly nothing suspicious about retrieving water and butter from the springhouse. As always, she was watchful as she approached the trees. It had seemed necessary since that man had cornered her by the creek several weeks ago. Seeing no one, she made her way through the trees that lined the creek rather than taking the more obvious wagon path.

She emerged just north of the springhouse and followed the bank south, past the crew's tents mostly hidden from her view until she thought she had gone too far. But there was Monroe, sitting on the remains of steps that led to an old footbridge. Emma hurried downstream until she reached him. He stood and took the bucket and the empty plate from her, setting them carefully next to the rotting steps.

"You're making me positively anxious for your news." Emma clasped her hands together as Monroe peered past her. "No one followed me. I was quite cautious."

Seemingly satisfied, he pulled a well-folded piece of paper from his pants pocket and handed it to her.

Emma tucked a wayward piece of hair behind her ear and took the paper. Reading it silently to herself, she tried to cull the meaning from it. It seemed as if Mr. Gilbert and his father were pleased with Monroe's progress and wanted to offer him something else. When she looked up, he was frowning.

"This is wonderful," she said, handing him the telegram. "You've worked hard for the company, and it hasn't gone unnoticed."

It was as if her praise had lit a candle inside of him, and his frown disappeared. "Thank you. It means more to hear that from you than from any other person."

The hair fell forward again, and Emma tucked it back, ducking her head in the process to hide her growing flush. "What does the last part of the message mean?"

"That's what I wanted to talk to you about." He took a step forward so that he was mere inches from her. "I haven't spoken with Gilbert yet, but it seems as if they want to offer me a job building another hotel."

Emma fought to pay attention to his words. Why was keeping her head clear so difficult whenever he was this close to her? "I'm so happy for you." She forced herself to breathe. "Truly. Your work speaks for itself."

"It is, but . . ."

Emma's heart sank as she realized what such an offer meant. She wanted to know his thoughts, know if him seeking her out—twice now—held any meaning, and here she was, about to find out. If he said what she hoped he might say, perhaps she could then finally tell him that she needed to continue earning an income, somehow. "But?"

He searched her face, and all she wanted was for him to take her in his arms and tell her that he would never leave her. But what did she expect? He wanted to craft a career in building, and that meant moving from place to place, never staying put for longer than a few months. Meanwhile, she had a contract to fulfill here at the Crest Stone Hotel.

"It means I'll have to leave."

"Where?" she asked in a whisper, unsure if she wanted to hear the answer.

"It's not clear. Not yet. I must speak with Gilbert, and then I'll know more."

Emma chewed on her lip, searching for what to say next. There were words on the tip of her tongue, ones she didn't dare speak aloud. *Take me with you.* She ached to hear him ask for her, down to the very marrow of her bones.

But could she go?

She bit down hard on her lip, drawing blood. It was foolish to worry on things that hadn't even occurred yet. He may not feel the same way. Or he may, but have no ideas to help her find a way to continue supporting her family.

"Leaving was inevitable. Once the hotel is finished, there's no legitimate reason for me to remain." Monroe hesitated, and then reached for her hands. Emma gave them gladly, reveling in the feel of his work-hardened fingers, and glad she'd left her gloves behind. He looked down at them, as if he was memorizing every line on her palm and every new freckle from the sun. Freckles that would make her mother blanch in horror. But if Monroe cared about freckles, he didn't show it.

"I know," she said, hardly daring to breathe.

"I . . ." Monroe trailed off, his eyes meeting hers. She tried in vain to read them. Resignation, some deep sadness—those were clear. But underneath . . . was that hope? It was almost as if he had something else he wanted to say.

"Well, ain't this an interesting turn of events?"

A jolt shot through Emma. She yanked her hands from Monroe's as she turned, something hot rising from her stomach and causing her entire body to tremble. Not ten feet away stood John Turner, the same man who had blackmailed Monroe out of his hard-earned money to keep their secret. Now he stood, arms crossed, hat tilted back, and his smile almost reaching his ears as he watched them.

But most surprising of all—at his side stood a woman.

Chapter Twenty-four

"Millie?" Emma almost breathed the name out.

The girl took a step backward, looking off toward the trees as if she didn't want to be there. But Turner reached out and pulled her forward. She tripped a little, but righted herself as he clutched her arm.

"Let her go," Monroe said, his voice clipped. He wanted to yank the girl from Turner's grasp and point her back in the direction of the house, but he knew he and Emma both would be better served if he stood where he was and heard Turner out.

Turner shook his head, although he dropped the girl's arm. "I don't believe you understand this situation, Mr. Hartley."

"What I understand is that you're here instead of rousing the men to start work. And that you're pulling this poor girl around as if she were a dog you didn't like."

Turner laughed without any shred of mirth. "You overstep your authority here, Hartley."

Monroe swallowed back the anger that threatened to breach. "I overstep nothing. I'm the boss of this operation. If you want to keep your position, I suggest you leave the lady alone and return to your work."

Turner made no move to leave, but instead took a few steps forward. "You forget I'm keeping your secret. And now, thanks to my dear friend Miss Sinclair, I believe I'm finished with that."

"With what, exactly?" Monroe said the words to buy time more than anything else. If Turner intended to take his knowledge to McFarland, Monroe needed every precious minute to figure out what to do.

"Why don't you tell them, Miss Sinclair?" Turner shifted his body to allow them to better see the girl behind him.

Miss Sinclair moved closer to Monroe. Her face had gone pale, and all he wanted to do was guide her to Emma, who would keep her safe and out of the way of men like Turner.

"Millie?" Turner prompted, impatience tinging the edges of his voice.

The girl twisted her hands together and looked to Turner. He nodded, and she moved her gaze to Monroe, then Emma. "This morning, I heard someone go out of doors before the sun had even risen. I was curious, so I followed. When I came to the yard behind the house, I saw someone scurry around the side of the barn. So I followed her and discovered Miss Daniels meeting clandestinely with Mr. Hartley. They spoke of meeting again later, and he kissed her."

When she stopped speaking, Turner laid a hand on her arm, and she gave him a grateful smile as color rose to her cheeks again. Emma stared at Millie, disbelief written from her forehead to her chin.

"And now," Turner said in a slow drawl, "Miss Sinclair came to the springhouse to retrieve butter that Miss Daniels said she had intended to bring back thirty minutes ago. Instead, she saw Miss Daniels' footprints headed south. Worried about Miss Daniels, Miss Sinclair followed her. When she arrived, she found this." He gestured at Monroe and Emma, a sneer on his face. "Clearly, Miss Sinclair, Miss Daniels has been seduced by this good-for-nothing builder. Why else would they be meeting in private? Why else would his hands be all over her? This is something Mr. McFarland and Mrs. Ruby should know about, don't you think?"

Emma gasped. Monroe took a step forward, ready to show the man exactly what he thought of his speculations. But one step was all he got to take, because just then, Turner reached for something at his hip.

"I'd stay right there, Hartley." Turner held an old Colt Army revolver in his hand, pointed directly at Monroe.

He stopped short and pulled Emma behind him, never taking his eyes from the barrel of Turner's revolver. "Just what do you intend to do with that?"

"Not a thing so long as you do as you're told." His eyes slid sideways until they found Emma peeking out from behind Monroe. "You understand me, don't you, Miss Daniels?"

Emma's hand, which still held on to Monroe's arm, trembled. He wanted nothing more than to knock that revolver out of Turner's hand and beat him to a pulp. Inwardly, he cursed himself for leaving his own guns back in his tent. Although it wasn't as if he wore them on a daily basis. He was no gunslinger, and the threats in this valley were few.

Until now.

"John?" Miss Sinclair spoke up, her voice shaky.

"Go," he said. "Tell Mrs. Ruby and Mr. McFarland what you know."

She stood rooted to the spot, her pale eyes locked on the gun. "But what are you going to do?"

"Nothing," he said, "so long as Hartley does as I ask."

When she made no move to leave, he grabbed her arm and shook her. "Go on, before you're missed."

She turned and ran, even as Emma called out her name again.

"Keep your mouth shut," Turner said as Emma called again for Miss Sinclair.

Monroe clenched his hands into fists, trying to keep his anger in check. "I know why you're doing this. You want more than money—you want my position."

Turner shifted but held the gun steady. "Ain't you the smart one?"

Monroe didn't acknowledge the question. "What isn't clear to me, though, is why you've involved the ladies."

"Does it matter?"

"It does." The anger in his voice must have been evident, as Emma squeezed his arm. At her touch, he took a breath and steadied himself before speaking again. "Miss Daniels seems to simply be a casualty of your scheme, but why Miss Sinclair?"

"Having the story come from both of them lends it more credence," Emma said softly from behind him. "Particularly when there is no clear connection between them. Isn't that true, Mr. Turner?" Her voice shook a fraction when she said the man's name, but that was the only indication that she felt any fear. His Emma, brave as a bear facing down a pack of hunters.

Turner bestowed an amused look on Emma, but nodded. "Perhaps I should've chosen you instead of Miss Sinclair."

Monroe threw an arm back protectively and fixed Turner with a look he hoped told the man exactly what he'd do right now if Turner didn't have that revolver pointed at him.

Turner chuckled. "Ease off, Hartley. I've got no interest in your woman."

"You've debased Miss Sinclair for no purpose other than your own personal gain." Monroe spat the words at the man.

"Why do you care? She's nothing to you."

Monroe's fists clenched harder. If he moved fast enough, he just might be able to catch Turner off guard. All he had to do—

"I can't . . ." Emma pushed past him, one of her arms outstretched, the other clutching at her throat. "Can't . . . breathe."

Fear rocked Monroe's entire body. If Turner had caused Emma any pain, he'd pay. He'd pay more than he could have ever imagined. Monroe reached for Emma, his arms encircling her waist. Her weight dropped against him, and he ground his heels into the soft dirt of the bank to keep them both upright.

"What's wrong with her?" Turner asked.

Emma swayed a little, her eyes fluttering closed.

"I don't know." Monroe's voice veered toward the frantic. He needed to remain calm. He couldn't help her if he let the same frenzy he'd felt when Colette became sick take him over again. He focused on the weight of her in his arms—her very alive body warm against him.

Slowly, reason returned as he helped Emma remain upright in his arms. She was still conscious, her eyes opening just a little. "Emma? Lie down." Monroe tried to ease her to the ground when she turned in his arms, just enough to shield her face from Turner.

Go, she mouthed at him before closing her eyes and grabbing at her throat again.

It was an act. He had to redouble his hold to keep from dropping her, stunned as he was. He wanted to yell at her, make her know how much she'd scared him. But he couldn't, because this woman—this amazing woman—scared him to death in order to save them both. He eased her to the ground and then, quick as a cat, leapt on Turner.

The man tumbled backward, the gun flying from his hand. Monroe pinned him to the ground, even as Turner thrashed and fought him. They were evenly matched, and Monroe didn't know how long he could keep Turner down.

"Run!" he shouted to Emma.

She scrambled to her feet but hesitated. "I want to help."

"I've got him. Go now! You need to reach the house before she does." The words came in puffs of air. It was taking all his effort to hold Turner down as the edge Monroe had from his surprise attack wore off.

Emma ran, straight through the trees. Turner bucked suddenly, knocking Monroe sideways. Monroe hit the ground. Turner stood, but before he could lunge for the gun, Monroe grabbed his ankle, pulling him down again. All he had to do was stall the man long enough for Emma to get to the house. Turner stretched his arm out, inching his fingers toward the revolver. Monroe rose. He pinned one knee in Turner's back. Then he reached out and grabbed at the man's shirtsleeve, pulling at it.

He yanked Turner's arm back far enough he couldn't reach the handle of the revolver. Monroe held him there for what felt like forever, muscles burning and straining, as Turner sputtered and cursed at him. Finally, when he estimated enough time had passed, he jumped off Turner with the little energy he had left and snagged the revolver. Turner was right behind him, but Monroe flipped around and held the weapon out in front of him. Turner stopped short, hands outstretched.

Breathing hard, Monroe held the gun as steady as he could. "It's done now. There's nothing for us to fight over."

Turner watched him through narrowed eyes as his chest rose and fell.

"Go." Monroe nudged the revolver toward the wagon path. "I won't stop you."

Turner kept his eyes on the gun as he tested Monroe's words by stepping sideways. When Monroe didn't shoot, he took off at full speed.

Monroe let the gun fall to his side. All he hoped was that Mrs. Ruby and the McFarlands found Emma more believable than Miss Sinclair. Nothing either he or Turner could say would change things now. But he couldn't leave Emma to fend for herself against both Miss Sinclair and his foreman. He tucked the revolver into the back of his trousers and took off after Turner. The man had perhaps a quarter mile on him, but Monroe was faster, even though his lungs burned with the effort.

By the time Turner reached the house, Monroe was right behind him. Turner didn't knock; instead he tore the door open. Monroe grabbed hold of it before Turner could shut it in his face.

Inside, they were met with sober looks. Mrs. Ruby and McFarland and his wife formed a semicircle around the two girls. Emma turned, and her eyes glistening with unshed tears. Her hands were clenched at her sides, and Monroe knew.

This was not going in their favor.

Chapter Twenty-five

I t took all of Emma's strength to keep the tears from leaving her eyes. It took even more for her not to fall into Monroe's arms the second he burst through the door behind that snake, Mr. Turner. Winded and disheveled, Monroe looked more handsome than ever to her, but she knew that to the McFarlands and Mrs. Ruby, he looked every inch the cad who had defiled her reputation.

Nails digging into her palms, she turned back to the women and man who held her future—and Monroe's—in their hands. Mrs. Ruby looked at her with barely disguised disappointment. According to Millie, Emma and Monroe had been found in all sorts of compromising positions, none of which Millie felt comfortable describing to the others. Despite Emma's protestations, she couldn't deny that she and Monroe had formed a connection. To deny that would be to deny her very heart.

"Perhaps the gentlemen can shed some light on this situation," Mrs. McFarland said. She'd seemed more sympathetic to Emma than the others, and now she appeared to eye Monroe with hope. "Mr. Hartley?"

Monroe took a breath. Emma wanted so badly to reach for his hand, to let him know how much she cared for him, and that nothing anyone said could change that. To let him know she'd stand here with him and accept whatever decision was reached. But she didn't. If there was even a shred of hope left for either one of them, she couldn't ruin it. Her family depended on it. Monroe's livelihood depended on it.

Monroe glanced at her, his eyes darker than usual. She couldn't read them, couldn't tell what he was thinking. He turned back to the others. "I care very deeply for Miss Daniels. I apologize for any wrongdoing. My intentions with Miss Daniels were nothing but good, despite what others may say."

Mr. McFarland huffed, his face red. "You were informed, after that incident at the hotel, to stay away from her."

Mrs. McFarland laid a hand on her husband's arm, but to no avail. Monroe held Mr. McFarland's gaze, and Emma warmed with pride. This man would never be cowed.

"I know, sir. I have no defense. I should have left Miss Daniels alone. Please know that from here on out, I will do so."

Emma stared. She was so certain that he was about to lay his soul bare back at the creek, just before Mr. Turner and Millie had appeared. He was saying this to salvage their positions, that was all. It had to be. And if she had any hope at all of saving her job here, she needed to do the same.

"I fear it's too late for such promises," Mrs. Ruby chimed in. "Mr. Turner, have you anything to add?"

Mr. Turner stepped forward. He'd composed his face into something that resembled concern.

"I am sorry to say that I, too, have witnessed Mr. Hartley and Miss Daniels together in . . . shall we say, romantic embraces? . . . on more than one occasion."

Mrs. Ruby pressed her lips together as she glanced at Emma again. It was hopeless, Emma knew that now. After what Mr. Turner said, her fate was sealed. Mr. McFarland all but glared at Monroe, while his wife frowned sympathetically.

"The first time I discovered this indiscretion, I spoke with Mr. Hartley. I reminded him of his duty to his work and to Mr. Gilbert, but he pushed me aside. There wasn't much else I could do, given he is my superior. He all but threatened me if I should speak of this to you, Mr. McFarland." Turner looked every inch the sorrowful employee. It made Emma's stomach turn to hear him disparage Monroe in such a way.

Monroe's hands tightened into fists, but that was the only clue to how angry he was at Turner. Emma hated to see him in such a demeaned position. She wanted nothing more than to slap Turner across the face and expose him for the charlatan he was.

"Despicable," Mrs. Ruby said as she glared at Monroe.

"It isn't true," Emma said. She couldn't help it. She could no longer stand there quietly and listen to these lies. Her feelings for Monroe ran too deep to let them rip him apart like this.

"Miss Daniels, you've had your moment." Mr. McFarland's warning was enough to silence her.

Turner shot her a sad look, almost as if he was sorry for her. It was an act, and Emma burned for everyone to know it.

"Mr. Turner, you may continue." Mr. McFarland gestured at him.

Mr. Turner cleared his throat and turned his hat in his hands. "Just this morning, I fell upon a scene that upset me. Miss Sinclair had discovered the two of them together again, when I gather Miss Daniels was supposed to be fetching butter. When I arrived, to get water for my crew, I found Mr. Hartley all but threatening Miss Sinclair. Naturally, I could not stand for such a thing." He looked almost lovingly at Millie, who brightened all over at the attention.

Emma understood now, and if she wasn't so angry at Millie, she'd feel sorry for her. Mr. Turner had used the girl. Who knew what he had promised her, but that look she gave him spoke volumes. She believed he loved her. Emma ground her teeth to keep from lashing out at Mr. Turner. He was truly the devil in disguise, willing to use anyone to further his own desires. He had no plans to court Millie. The poor girl would end up heartbroken at best, and ruined at worst.

"I was able to keep Mr. Hartley at bay while Miss Sinclair ran for safety, but once she left, he brandished his weapon at me. I managed to get it away from him, but then, as you can see, he took my own gun and then held me to the ground so Miss Daniels could attempt to discredit Miss Sinclair here." He gestured at the dirt on his clothing.

"I've heard enough." Mr. McFarland crossed his arms.

His wife placed a hand on his shoulder. "Mr. Hartley, you said you had nothing but good intentions with Miss Daniels?"

"That is true," Monroe said, his voice perfectly measured.

"Well, perhaps if . . . ?" She didn't finish the sentence, but instead looked to Monroe.

Emma's breath caught in her throat. She thought she knew what Mrs. Mc-Farland was hoping for. If Monroe asked for her hand, then perhaps he could at least keep his place here. It wouldn't help Emma's family, but . . . her entire body warmed at the thought of becoming Monroe's wife.

Monroe's eyes were on Mrs. McFarland. It was quiet for a moment—so quiet, Emma was sure the entire room could hear her thoughts.

"I meant no harm to Miss Daniels, I assure you," Monroe said.

It was silent again. The blood drained from Emma's face. She tried to catch his eye, but he still faced forward. He wasn't going to ask for her. He didn't want her.

Through the window, the sun beat down and the yellow wildflowers danced in the breeze. Out there, she could run and run and run until she disappeared, into the mountains or down the creek. Outside, she could sob to her heart's content, let all the pain that was bottled up inside her flow out.

All of this time . . . why had he led her on? She would lose her place here, and he was all she had left. But now that he had publicly denied her, she had nothing.

She clutched her arms around herself and swayed a little. Out of nowhere, Caroline emerged from the doorway. She wrapped an arm around Emma to steady her, and without a word, began to lead her to the stairs.

"You will pack your things, Emma," Mrs. Ruby said, stern but with a hint of sadness tinging her voice. "Mr. McFarland will take you to Cañon City in the morning for the train."

The train. Home. There was nowhere else for her to go now. She had failed Mrs. Ruby, failed her family, failed herself. And for what? A broken heart. She couldn't even look at Monroe again. It would hurt too much. All she hoped was that by the time she emerged downstairs again, he'd be gone. He could at least leave her with her dignity, even though he'd taken everything else.

She let Caroline lead her up the stairs, away from the eyes boring into her back.

Chapter Twenty-six

After Emma's friend had taken her upstairs, McFarland had led Monroe and Turner outside, away from the ladies. Monroe looked off to the snow-capped Sangre de Cristos in the west, a magnificent backdrop to the hotel he had built.

Had. That was over now.

McFarland confirmed it when he ordered Turner to take charge of the entire crew.

"Big Jim would be a better choice," Monroe said. It was the truth. Not only was the man more trustworthy, he'd had years more experience with building than Turner, even if he didn't have quite the ability to keep the crew organized. Why he hadn't chosen Big Jim as his foreman instead of Turner, the lying scoundrel, was beyond him.

"You don't question my decisions," McFarland snapped at him.

An ugly smile crossed Turner's face before he thanked McFarland and headed up the hill to the hotel.

"I only sought to ensure success with this venture. I put my blood and my heart into this place," Monroe said as he watched Turner disappear into the camp.

"I believe that," McFarland said, a little softer. "I'm disappointed, Hartley."

Monroe sighed. "You're only doing what you need to. No reason to feel bad about it."

"It's not that."

Monroe turned to study the older man.

"If you'd done what was right, chances are I could've convinced Gilbert to keep you on to finish the place."

What was right. That sick feeling Monroe'd had when he fought back the urge to claim Emma as his wife in front of all of them made its way back up his throat. How he'd wanted to ask for her right then! But he couldn't, he knew that. It would be selfish, offering everything to her and then expecting her to roam the country with him as he went from job to job. So he'd kept quiet and watched as her heart broke in front of his eyes.

He'd never felt like a worse person than he had at that moment. Not even when he'd lost his sister. Not even when Colette had succumbed to his selfish pursuits.

He'd broken Emma. Even worse, he'd done it in front of everyone they knew. He shouldn't have ever pursued her. If he was any sort of decent man, he'd have left her alone.

"You aren't the man I thought you were," McFarland said.

He deserved that. He let the words sink in. He wasn't worthy of Emma, anyhow. He would've killed her the same way he'd killed Colette. Even thinking he could have a second chance was wrong. It was selfish, and God knew that, and so he'd punished Monroe. Now he was free to follow his desire to create buildings.

Alone.

McFarland watched him for a moment. "I'll give you a good reference, although I probably shouldn't. You've done excellent work here. I'll let Gilbert know I've had to terminate your employment, but I won't say why."

"Thank you." Monroe adjusted his hat and the hotel, grand and soaring at the top of the hill, looked down on him.

If only he could've seen it through.

IT WAS NEARING MIDNIGHT when Monroe latched his one remaining saddlebag onto Pender as the horse nudged his arm. He hadn't brought much with him to start—some clothes, a blanket, a few mementos. All of it fit neatly into the saddlebag. He'd never purchased a new one after using his to fix Emma's trunk. He'd hesitated a moment with one last item—the creased page from Emma's poetry book. The one she'd given him a few weeks ago, on top of the hill north of Crest Stone. One perfect moment.

He clutched the fragile page in his palm, the lemon scent of her flooding his mind. Her shy smile when he complimented her, the blush she'd had when her trunk fell open the day they first met, the feel of her soft skin beneath his hands. He wished now that he'd kissed her. He'd held back, not wanting to scare her, and now . . . they would never see each other again. She hated him, he was certain. It was all his doing, but it was necessary. He only wished he could have done it in a way that didn't hurt her so much.

He placed the page into the bag and latched it closed.

There was one thing left to do before he caught a few hours' sleep and left at first light.

He grabbed a lamp and the small bottle of whiskey Big Jim had given him a while back and made his way across the camp toward the hotel. It was still now, all the men having turned in an hour or more ago. The house below was dark. It was only him and the hotel.

Monroe grasped the doorknob on one of the imposing front doors and pushed it open. The door swung in with barely a creak, and he smiled. He'd done good work.

He ran his fingers over the chair rail that lined the entire large lobby. The wood was smooth and polished to a sheen, he knew without even seeing it. Excellent craftsmanship. All done under his watchful eye.

It physically hurt him to leave this project undone. How he'd dreamed of the day when the first guests would arrive. He'd imagined them stepping down from the train, mouths agape and eyes wide to take in the magnificence of this structure—*his* hotel. They'd move through the building in awe, appreciating the fine work of everything from the doorframes to the floor to the placement of the lighting.

And he'd stand by proudly, ready to take on his next assignment with Emma by his side.

Monroe stopped and knocked his forehead against the wall.

Emma.

He hit the wall with his fist. He hadn't intended to think of her here. He'd wanted only to focus on this incredible place he'd created. But there she was, at every step.

Her small hand grasping the hole where the doorknob should have been in the powder room. Her eyes roving the delicate work of the doorframe. Her mind picturing a settee here and a lamp there.

Monroe sank to the floor against the long lobby desk. He'd overseen its creation from start to finish. He pulled the cork from the bottle and held the amber liquid at eye level. Then he sighed and recorked it. He didn't even deserve to drink. The only thing he deserved was to sit here and remember what he'd done.

He was too cowardly to even look at her when he'd refused to ask for her. He didn't want to see the disappointment in her eyes. All the hope that he'd placed there and then wiped away in the course of seconds.

But he couldn't have proposed to her without explaining what that meant, without telling her exactly what had happened to Colette and how she would've faced the same fate. If she'd said yes, picturing a home somewhere for the two of them, and then the reality was moving from place to place, how would that have been fair to her? It was better this way. She'd be alive, even if she did hate him.

He'd be on his way at first light. She would forget about him in time.

He only hoped he would never forget about her.

Chapter Twenty-seven

A few lamps still flickered in the midnight black of Cañon City. Emma stood at the curtain of the window overlooking the street. This hotel room wasn't much, but it would suffice for one short night. The plan had been for Mr. McFarland to take her to Cañon City in the morning, but after packing her things and drying her eyes, Emma wanted to put it all behind her as soon as possible.

Caroline asked her to stay the night, with Penny and Dora and even the new girls chiming in. They'd miss her, they said, and they wanted to keep her company. Besides, she shouldn't be alone tonight, not after everything that had happened. But Emma was determined. The sooner she could leave, the sooner she'd be able to put all the memories in the past where they belonged. She was going home, and it was time she faced that fact.

Despite the late hour, people were still awake on the street below. Light and music poured from a saloon down the road, and here and there, a man who'd imbibed a bit too much lurched from its door and wound his way down the street.

Sighing, Emma pushed away from the window and crossed the room to the wardrobe where she'd hung her travel dress. She made another effort at brushing the dust off, but it was useless. She closed the door and gathered her long nightgown in her hand. Her braid swayed at her back as she recrossed the room to douse the lamp. It was too quiet when she got into bed, even with the music outside. An ache tore at her insides.

It wasn't just Monroe she missed—at least the Monroe she'd thought she'd known—but her friends too. Caroline's whispered prayers, Penny's light snores, and Dora's quiet mutterings in her sleep. She'd grown as used to them as she had to her sisters. She wondered what would become of them. Would Caroline retreat back into herself? She hoped that Penny would continue to draw her out, so long as she could stay out of trouble herself. And Dora . . . Emma had befriended her, and the girl was nice enough, but still withdrawn, almost as if some great sadness hung over her life. Emma regretted not getting to know her better.

And Monroe. Always Monroe. Emma turned to her side, bunched up the feather pillow beneath her head, and squeezed her eyes shut. It was no use. His name clawed at her heart and shredded her soul. She'd been so certain that he was picturing a future for them, together. But when the time came for him to declare himself, he didn't. She was too empty—too drained—to even try to put her feelings into poetry.

It had been a mistake, giving him any of her attention. She should have pushed him away that very first day when she'd arrived. Instead, she'd fallen for him, completely taken by his wit and the way his eyes lit up when he looked at her. His smile had been her undoing. If not for that, she'd still have her position and her friends.

Now she had nothing but memories.

It's for the best, she told herself again. Even if she wasn't a Gilbert Girl, she still had to earn money to support her family. Marrying Monroe wouldn't have changed that fact. In fact, it would've made it harder. She'd had her big adventure out West, enjoyed her independence, breathed in the air from under an untouched sky, and lost her heart.

Her heart would heal with time, that she knew from losing Papa. The dull ache might always be there, but the gash that left her in ruins now would grow smaller each day.

She'd go back home and do her duty.

But one thing she knew for certain—as whole as her heart might one day become, she'd never love anyone the way she'd loved Monroe.

Chapter Twenty-eight

Emma ran toward him in a dress as blue as the Colorado sky. Her hair had come loose from its binding, and tendrils flew in the wind as she moved closer. Her laugh flooded all of his senses, warming him up and making everything around them sharper than it should be. He caught her flush against his chest and wrapped his arms around her delicate frame. Breathing in the lemon scent of her hair, he knew nothing would ever be better than this. No building would ever be as magnificent, no commendations would ever make him so proud, nothing could be greater than Emma in his arms. His forever.

As he looked down at her sweet face, her laugh disappeared. She frowned at him, and some aching need surged through his body—lonely, bereft, it gutted his heart.

"Why did you leave me?" she asked.

"Leave? I'm right here." He reached for a piece of her hair to push it behind her ear, but his hand sailed right through her.

"I miss you," the ghost Emma said. "I love you, still."

He tried to grab on to her waist, but it was no longer solid under his hand. She shimmered, a mirage misplaced here in the mountains.

Then she was gone.

Monroe jerked awake, gasping for air. The full whiskey bottle clattered to the wooden floor where he lay sprawled. He rubbed at his face. It was still dark outside through the windows flanking the front doors, and the lamp sputtered dimly at his side.

His heart finally slowed, and it was a relief until he realized the dream was true.

Monroe groaned and bumped the back of his head against the fine dark woodwork of the lobby desk. Across from him, the delicate floral wallpaper spoke of happy times to come in this hotel he'd built. But it was all meaningless without the one thing that mattered to him most. And that thing wasn't a hotel or anything else he could create with his mind and his hands. It was Emma.

And he'd let her go.

Even worse, he'd let her believe he'd never loved her. He'd been a fool. A complete fool. McFarland had tried to tell him, but he'd been too dense to understand. A hotel would never make him feel like the man he'd been before Colette died. But Emma would. She already had.

He had to get her back. Even if it meant giving up his dream of building. He'd do anything for her.

He'd had it all backwards before. The decision wasn't his. It was hers. How they chose to live their lives, whether it was following his dream or putting down roots in one place, wasn't his choice to make. All he had to do was ask her, and then let her decide.

And he'd need to gather the courage to tell her about Colette.

Monroe grabbed the lamp and bottle before standing. Emma wasn't leaving until morning. He'd wait out front of the house for her. Provided he could convince McFarland that now he planned to do the right thing, he'd be able to talk to her. First, he'd apologize for being so cruel. Then he'd ask her to marry him. After she said yes—how he prayed she'd say yes, although he'd deserve it if she turned him down—only then would they discuss how to live their lives. Whatever she wanted, he wanted too.

With renewed determination, he strode out of the hotel and back toward his tent. He'd grab a few hours of sleep and then see Emma.

He'd never felt so sure of anything.

Chapter Twenty-nine

"Now that we're alone, will you tell us the truth about why you left?" Lily sat on the bed next to Emma.

Emma paused in relatching the trunk. She should've known she couldn't hide anything from Lily. This was the sister who could tell she'd fibbed to Mama about getting into trouble at school when she was ten. If Lily could see that, then it would've been impossible for her to miss the greatest sorrow Emma had borne since their father's death.

"What do you mean?" Grace asked as she took the trunk from Emma and stowed it at the foot of the bed.

Lily said nothing. She simply looked at Emma, her big green eyes waiting for an explanation. Grace sat on the bed opposite, the one she shared with Mama. This new apartment was so small that the four of them had to sleep in one room, with barely space between the two beds, while Joseph slept in the kitchen. It reminded Emma of sharing a room with her friends in Crest Stone.

Emma sighed, her eyes on the trunk. Monroe had fixed it, that very first night, after laying eyes on almost everything she owned. She hadn't seen him that night when he brought her trunk back, but she'd spent far too long running her fingers over the fine leatherwork and imagining him piecing it all together. Imagining the way his dark hair fell into his face, the way he'd run his hand over his chin as he thought hard about something. That cavern inside her opened anew and unshed tears stung her eyes. She should've known she couldn't have kept any of this a secret from her sisters.

"It was not as I told you." She picked up the lace coverlet that had been on her bed for as long as she could remember. The delicate cloth sat between her fingers as it always did, and something about that familiarity made it easier for her to breathe. That was possibly the most jarring aspect of her return home—how choked the humid summer air was here with smoke and horse manure and unwashed people. She had never noticed it until she left, and now it was hard to breathe it in and not remember the fresh, cool breeze of Colorado—air that held the promise of everything in its whisper.

"Was it horrid?" Grace asked timidly. "You said it didn't suit you. Was it worse than you let on? Were they cruel to you?"

"Oh no, it wasn't anything of the sort. I worked hard, as did the other girls, but it was good, fair work. We enjoyed our Sundays off, and we had time to converse and relax. The girls were wonderful, and Mrs. Ruby was kind." Emma pushed the cloth between her fingers, letting the knots of it dig into her skin as the emotion threatened to choke her again. "It was . . . Oh, I don't know how to tell you."

Lily laid a hand on her arm. "I told you all about how mad I was over Mr. Carrothers. Surely you can tell us of your great romantic adventure out West."

Emma felt her cheeks grow hot. Lily saw far more than she'd let on at first. "How did you know?"

Lily laughed. "Please, Em. I've never seen anyone so sad and yet so caught up in her own daydreams. Save for myself when Mr. Carrothers mentioned to Mama that I had hair prettier than silk and then became a priest instead of courting me."

Emma smiled, though it almost pained her to do so. Lily's infatuation with their neighbor last year had been quite the entertainment for Emma and Grace.

And so, she told them about Monroe. About how full of life he was, how witty and charming, how handsome and hard-working, how dedicated he was in his dream of becoming the great American builder. And then how much he had captivated her. How sure she was that he felt the same . . . until it became evident he didn't.

When she finished, Grace held one of her hands while Lily had wrapped an arm around her. She leaned into them the same way she had with Penny and Caroline right before she'd left.

"He is a beast," Grace said, with all the surety of her fifteen years. "He was never worthy of you. And if I ever see him, I'll tell him so."

Lily said nothing. It took Emma a few more moments to fully compose herself, but when she did, she turned just slightly so she could see Lily's face. Her sister was deep in thought. Emma gave her another moment and then finally could stand it no longer.

"What are you thinking so hard about?"

Lily looked up at her. "Something doesn't fit together."

"How so?" Emma asked as she and Grace both stared at their sister. "It felt clear to me."

"From what you've told us, he seemed quite taken with you."

Emma nodded. She'd believed it—to her detriment.

"What did he say when you met him that morning by the creek?" Lily asked.

Emma pulled away from her sister's embrace in order to see her better. "He told me that he might have an offer from Mr. Gilbert to build another hotel. He seemed to hesitate, though. As if something was on his mind, but that's when we were interrupted. At first, I thought he was going to confess his true feelings, but then . . ." She couldn't bring herself to speak about how he'd rejected her in front of everyone.

"I wonder what he wanted to say . . ." Lily said this more to herself than to Emma.

"Maybe he was going to ask you to marry him." Grace's voice was breathy and high.

Emma shook her head. The thought had crossed her mind too, but now it made no sense. If he'd planned to ask for her then, why not later?

"No," Lily agreed. "But perhaps there was something else. Something that was making him hesitate before asking for your hand."

Could that be why he'd rebuffed her completely when he had the opportunity to ask for her? Emma's mind raced through the possibilities. "I can't think of anything."

"That must be it, though," Lily said.

It made perfect sense. "It would have to be something he was not comfortable asking me in front of everyone else. But if that was true, why didn't he come find me that evening?"

Lily reached for her hand. "I don't know. Maybe he felt as if he had already messed everything up too badly?"

Emma pressed her lips together. It was possible. But what was impossible was everything somehow righting itself now. It was too late. She'd already left, and he'd never come to find her. She drew a ragged breath. It was time she took the first step forward and put the past behind her. "Shall we go look for work tomorrow?"

Lily looked at her with such sadness in her eyes that Emma couldn't keep the tears from her own eyes. "I suppose."

"I'm so sorry," Emma whispered. "I wanted so badly to be a Gilbert Girl, to keep you both from having to work. And now I've made a mess of it all." Tears streaked down her cheeks. Her sweet younger sisters, full of sunshine and health. What would they become once they were closed into a factory from early morning until night?

Grace set her jaw. "We don't fault you. Not one little bit."

"You made such a sacrifice for us," Lily added. "Don't feel badly that it didn't work out." She reached up and wiped the tears from Emma's face.

"We're sisters," Grace said. "We'll pull our family through this together."

Emma swallowed hard and smiled at them.

"And who knows," Lily said. "Mr. Carrothers may renounce the priesthood any day now and come ask for me. We'll be gloriously rich." She patted her hair and stuck her nose in the air.

Emma giggled through her tears as Grace laughed so hard she nearly fell from the bed.

"Come, let's get some rest," Emma finally said. But as she lay in bed and tried to think about how they would go about finding work tomorrow, all she could see was the wide open valley she'd left behind. And Monroe.

Could it be true, what Lily had suggested? Was it possible there was something that held him back from asking for her? She had left so quickly. Perhaps he'd come to speak with her the next morning, only to find her gone.

She turned onto her side, toward the small window with a view of the stars overhead. It was pointless to worry on it. After all, there was nothing she could do now. Monroe was part of her past.

But as she closed her eyes, his face was all she saw.

Chapter Thirty

Monroe had barely slept the night after he and Emma were dismissed, but when he'd gone to the house in the morning, Emma was gone. Mrs. Mc-Farland had informed Monroe that her husband had taken Emma to Cañon City during the night. By the time Monroe had come looking for her, Emma was already on a train for Denver.

Monroe felt as if that train had run over him, hearing those words. He'd debated his options—he could ride to Denver to try to catch her, but it would be nigh on impossible to find new horses along the way and still make it before she left the city. He could write her a letter. Or he could board the next train and chase her clear back to Kentucky. He'd chosen the latter, which was how he now found himself standing, bewildered, in a depot in Louisville. At least he'd had the foresight to throw water on his face and comb his hair at the last stop in Indiana so he would not waste precious time here trying to pull himself together.

Now all he had to do was find her.

The entire way here, he'd searched his memory for anything Emma had said about her childhood home. It was near Broadway. It was red brick. And the family no longer lived there. It was not much to go on, but Monroe was determined to find a neighbor who might know where the Daniels family had relocated.

Outside the depot, the city chugged and churned, the sky filled with smoke from numerous factories, and the carriages moved to and fro. A line of hansom cabs bordered the depot, and Monroe made his way to the first one.

"This is Broadway," the driver said, a cigar in his mouth. He gestured to the wide street ahead of them. "All you need to do is walk a little ways east of here. You'll know when you're there."

Monroe gave the man a coin in thanks and started off in the direction he'd pointed. Immediately across the street, a hotel beckoned tired passengers from the depot. He moved quickly past it, so quickly, in fact, that he had to force himself to slow down unless he wanted to meet Emma drenched in sweat. That was looking inevitable, anyway. Monroe tugged at his collar to loosen it. The heat here clung to every inch of his skin, sealing it with a sheen of perspiration.

Not far from the depot, the scenery changed into fine houses and thriving businesses. People in fashionable clothes walked at a sedate pace past him, while even more journeyed past in carriages down the street. He turned at a cross street and let the imposing homes stare down at him. Glancing up at the nearest one, a three-story white house flanked with columns, he wondered at the wealth Emma's family must have had before she'd lost her father. Next door stood one of many red brick homes. This was as good a place to start as any. He threw back his shoulders, fixed his tie, and stepped forward.

A harried maid answered the door at the first house. She looked down her nose at him, only after she glanced behind her as if his very presence took up too much of her precious time.

Monroe had never felt more out of place, but he held his ground. "Hello," he said. "Do you by chance know of a Miss Emma Daniels or the Daniels family? They lived nearby until very recently."

The woman adjusted her long white apron and narrowed her eyes at him.

Although he had spent time refreshing himself, under her steely gaze he became acutely aware of the fact that his clothing was not the height of fashion in this city. His coat had seen better days, and his suit was worn and wrinkled from travel.

The maid finally answered. "No, sir. I'm sorry, but I have not heard of such a family."

Although he'd wished to hear otherwise, he was also more than happy to move beyond her condescending perusal. He thanked her and went directly to the next home. One by one, he stopped at each house, asking after the Daniels family. After exhausting a block of homes on both sides, he moved to the next cross street. An hour passed, then two, then three. He'd worked his way three blocks down Broadway on both sides. Frustration crept up inside him, but he refused to give up. If he had to knock on every door in this city, he would.

At the next cross street, he turned right and stopped at the first house, a friendly-looking whitewashed brick home. The front door opened just as he'd climbed the steps leading up from the street.

"Oh!" A young woman paused, parasol opened to guard against the sun, and an older woman directly behind her.

Monroe yanked the hat from his head and nodded at the ladies. "My apologies. I'm inquiring after a Miss Daniels, who lived nearby until recently. Might you know of her?"

"Emma?" The younger woman smiled. "I've known her for years."

Monroe wasn't certain he'd heard her correctly. "Pardon?"

"She's one of my oldest friends. But I thought she'd gone out West."

"It's a sad situation," the older woman said. Monroe pegged her as the girl's mother, judging from the similarities in their long, drawn faces. "It seems Mr. Daniels was not as well-off as he wanted everyone to believe. The mother fell ill, and the family ran low on funds. They moved house . . . oh, perhaps two months ago?" She looked to her daughter, who nodded.

Monroe gripped his hat tightly. He was so close. "You don't happen to know where the family moved?"

The daughter nodded. "They're in a small apartment on Campbell, near Adams. Second floor. It's not . . ." She shifted the tiny beaded reticule in her gloved hands.

"It isn't a desirable area of town," her mother finished.

"Is Emma home again?" the girl asked. "I visited her family once after she left, but I felt . . ." She looked again at her mother, but neither finished that time.

Monroe nodded. "Thank you for your help. I am indebted to you." He replaced his hat and turned to leave, then paused. "And yes, she is home again. Though perhaps not for long. You should visit her."

It took all of his self-control not to whistle as he moved down the brick street. It wasn't until he was almost back to Broadway that he realized he had no idea where he was headed. He walked swiftly down the road until he came to a mercantile, where he inquired after directions. It would not be a short walk, but with no other mode of transportation and no cabs within sight, walking was his only choice.

He walked and walked and walked, thinking he'd give anything for his horse right now. Perspiration dripped down his face and dashed any hope of looking calm and unhurried upon arrival. By the time he reached Emma's family's new neighborhood, the sun had set and he felt as if he'd journeyed for days.

At the corner of Adams and Campbell, one dimly lit ramshackle building matched the girl's description. Sucking in his breath, he removed his hat and smoothed his hair. Then he ran his hands down his coat and vest, brushing off any dirt.

The door that led to the second-floor apartments was locked. As he knocked, twenty different scenarios flew through his mind. Emma, answering the door and throwing herself into his arms as he vowed never to let her go again. Emma, spurning him and slamming the door in his face. One of Emma's sisters, insisting he explain why he'd acted the way he had. Or maybe her mother, frail and suspicious of this strange man asking for her daughter after dark.

When the door finally opened, he had to yank his mind back to the present. A girl stood in front of him, the very image of Emma, only with lighter hair. She held a lamp and had on a dress that looked worn at the edges but was neat as a pin, and her hair was pulled into a loose but flattering style. Her eyes narrowed for a moment as she took him in, and he braced himself for the words that matched that look. She placed one hand on her hip and said, "Mr. Monroe Hartley, I presume?" in a voice that spoke of fine upbringing but was frayed around the edges, as if she'd been awake longer than she should.

"I am. How did you know?"

She made a *hmpf* sound and moved not a muscle. "Have you come to your senses?"

He choked back a laugh. This girl spoke her mind, perhaps a bit too bluntly. But he couldn't help but admire someone who protected Emma the way he should have. "I have," he said in all seriousness. "I made a terrible mistake, as I assume Emma told you. And now I've come to right my wrongs. May I . . ." He peered around the girl. "May I see her, Miss Daniels? You are her sister, correct?"

She nodded. "I am. However, I'm afraid I can't help you. You see, my younger sister and I just returned from the factory only to find Emma gone. She disappeared from work earlier, and when we arrived here, we found she left us a note."

"A note?" Monroe raised his eyebrows. Goose bumps covered his arms under his shirtsleeves, even in this heat. He didn't have a very good feeling about this at all. "What do you mean? Is she all right?"

"Fine, I imagine. She's on a train back to Colorado, to find you."

Chapter Thirty-one

"I'm sorry, miss, but that route is a special run only right now. How about you come back in eight days? That's when the line is set to open for passengers." The older man pushed small, round spectacles farther up the bridge of his nose and smiled at her kindly.

"I see. Thank you." Emma pushed the last of her money back into her reticule. She already felt terrible enough about using this money for her own purposes, even though she was the one who earned it. At least the apartment had been paid for the month and the larder was full. She had resolved to pay these funds back to her family at the first opportunity—somehow.

But for now . . . She stood helplessly on the wooden plank sidewalk in Cañon City. She was so close to her destination, but with no way to get there. A carriage moved slowly through the street, the horses' legs covered in mud from a recent rain. If only she had a carriage, or even a buckboard wagon. She didn't know how to drive one, but she could figure it out.

"Excuse me, sir?" She turned back to the railroad man. "Where is the livery?"

"Down that way and left." He pointed.

Emma thanked him, picked up her skirts and tried to find a way across the street that wouldn't end up with *her* legs covered in mud. It was a semi-successful task. Her shoes did not fare well, but at least her legs were, for the most part, mud-free. She'd take a brush to her shoes later. Where she would find that brush, she didn't know. In fact, she didn't even know where she would sleep tonight. It wasn't as if the hotel would be open yet, even if she had enough money to lodge there.

She had to find Monroe. Once she did, she could then solve all of these other problems.

The livery was easy to locate. Inside, she wrinkled her nose at the scent of so many horses.

"'Afternoon, miss." A short, round man greeted her and then promptly looked behind her for a male companion.

She squared her shoulders, gripped her carpetbag even tighter, and looked the man straight in his beady little eyes. If she'd come to Colorado on her own, twice, she could go about finding transportation to Crest Stone with no chaperone. "I wish to procure a ride south to the Gilbert Company property in Crest Stone." When the man said nothing, she added, "I can pay."

He scratched at his protruding belly. "Lady, I don't know what to tell you. There's a stage that comes through nigh on twice a week, but that ain't till Tuesday. Why don't you wait till then?"

"I can't wait," Emma said. "Please, don't you know of someone who might take me? Today?"

He chuckled. "Truthfully? Not anyone I'd trust alone with my own sister."

Her face warmed, but she stood her ground.

"And it's three o'clock. To make a journey like that, you'd need to leave at dawn. Else your driver would be returning after dark."

Emma pushed her lips together. "Fine. Then what do you suggest? It's of the utmost importance that I arrive today."

He shook his head. "Miss, I don't know. Short of riding a horse, there ain't no way down there today. Now if you can wait—"

"A horse?"

"Now, I don't know about that. I was just saying—"

"I'd like to have a horse, then." She opened her reticule.

He looked her up and down. "You're dressed awful fine for this."

"Don't you worry about my clothing." She gave him a look that she hoped put the fear of God into him. This man was far too presumptuous.

Another man entered the wide open door behind them, leading a horse. The proprietor raised a hand in greeting, and Emma watched as the man disappeared into the darkness of the stable. If a man could ride for several hours at a time, so could she. It wasn't as if she had never been on horseback. It had simply been some time ago, and not for nearly as long. But she knew how to handle a horse.

"How much?" she asked. "To borrow a horse?"

"Now, I'm not in the habit of lending out horses," he said. "But if you're in the market to buy, I might be able to make you an offer. If you're dead set on doing this, that is. Which I advise against."

"How much to buy a horse, then?" She sent up a quick prayer that she'd have enough money. She was *so* close. There were only another forty or fifty miles between her and Monroe now.

The man studied her reticule, as if looking at it would tell him how much she had to spare. "Two hundred dollars."

Emma fought to keep her expression in check. Whatever made the man think she had that much? "I can give you seventy-five."

"Seventy-five?" He threw his head back and laughed, his large stomach heaving with the effort. "Lady, the only one I could part with for anywhere close to that is my old work horse, Samuel. And even he would cost you a hundred."

"I'll take him." Emma fished every last bill from her reticule and held it out to the man.

He stilled. "You serious?"

"Absolutely."

He ran a hand over the short, scraggly beard that covered his face. "Then perhaps you ought to see him first."

He led her back into the darkness. The small windows set high up on the walls were filthy and let little light through. Emma paused, uncertain if she should continue, until the man stopped to grab a lamp from a nail on the wall. When the flame took, the stable came into sharp relief. Horses peered over short wooden gates, straw lined the floor, and the smell grew even stronger back here. Emma's eyes watered at it as she followed the man to a small open area halfway through the stable. There, standing calmly and chewing on hay, stood the saddest-looking, slouch-backed, old gray gelding Emma had ever seen.

Emma closed her eyes and questioned her sanity. Then she opened them and spoke to the man. "I'll take him."

The man shook his head. She could see that he wanted to ask whether she was certain, but instead he untied the animal from its tether, grabbed an old set of tack hanging from the wall and an ancient saddle—"won't charge you for this," he muttered—put it on the horse, and handed her the reins. In turn, she handed him the money—the last she had left.

She tilted her head and looked at the horse. The horse looked back at her with droopy brown eyes. Then he snuffled and nosed at her sleeve.

"I'd offer you a hand, but . . ." The livery proprietor gestured at her skirts.

Emma glanced down. Her skirts were too long and too bulky to sit astride. She supposed she could ride aside, although that would grow uncomfortable quickly in this saddle. Yet another thing she hadn't really thought through.

"I'll figure it out," she said.

The man raised his scrawny eyebrows and laughed a little.

"Thank you for your help," Emma said, ignoring the laughter. She reached for the animal's reins, and then made her way to the front of the livery. Scanning this way and that down the street, she decided her best bet was to find a secluded place and deal with her skirts since she couldn't exactly hoist herself onto the horse to ride sidesaddle out of town without help.

She led the gelding to the west of town so as not to have to retrace her steps. He complied, and she decided she could at least be thankful for a cooperative horse, even if he might not have the stamina to make it all the way to Crest Stone. She was also thankful for having traveled this route several times with Mr. McFarland to attend services. At least she wouldn't become lost. She only had to pray the horse wouldn't collapse immediately.

About a mile or so after leaving town, a copse of trees flanking the Arkansas River beckoned. She tied the horse to a tree and set about doing the most unladylike thing she'd ever done in her life: stripping away the layers of petticoats under her skirt. One by one, she carefully piled them on the ground, until all she wore on her bottom half were her underthings, her stockings, and her skirt. She felt strangely light and free as she gathered up the discarded clothing.

Holding the fabric in her arms, Emma surveyed the area. She'd have to leave it all here since it wouldn't fit into her small carpetbag. Traveling alone, she'd had to leave her trunk behind at home. She could always come back to this spot and retrieve the clothing, so long as she hid it well. She finally decided upon a treacherous rock outcropping. Balancing herself on large, precariously placed stones, she buried the petticoats under even more rocks. When she finished, she dusted off her hands and smiled at her handiwork. She probably looked quite the sight right now without the petticoats under her dress, but she had more important things to worry about.

And with those on her mind, she used a rock as a stepping stool and mounted the horse. Clucking to him, she urged him along the river to the west.

Back to the hotel.

Back to Monroe.

Chapter Thirty-two

Monroe halted Pender and wiped the sheen of sweat from his forehead. It was nearly midnight, and he'd been riding hard since that evening when the last train of the day had brought him to Cañon City. He'd found his horse in the livery along with the most curious news. The livery owner recounted the tale of a young woman who'd impulsively bought his old work horse off him to ride herself southwest fifty miles—alone.

Monroe's stomach had lurched at the thought. He'd asked the man if the woman fit Emma's description, and although he knew she would, it didn't make hearing the confirmation any easier. She had several hours' lead on him, and his only hope was that she stuck to the main wagon path along the railroad tracks. If she strayed, he may never find her.

He'd made excellent time, and according to the landmarks he could see in the dark, he was but ten miles or so away from the hotel. He leaned forward and patted Pender's neck, then led him to the creek. He was a good horse, young and strong, otherwise he'd never have made it this far at such a fast pace. Even so, he knew he was pushing the animal's limits, and he felt terrible about it. "Not too much farther now," he said as the horse gulped the cool water. Even after he finished drinking, he didn't try any of his usual antics. Monroe climbed down and drank some himself even as he scoured the area for any signs of Emma.

There was nothing. There'd been nothing for miles. Either she hadn't left any trace, or she'd drifted off the path. He hoped for the former.

Back on Pender, he pushed the horse to speed again. The night air was oddly warm, air he'd more often felt when working at the ranch out on the plains. Here, it generally cooled at night, even after the hottest day. But he was thankful it was not that heavy, humid air that almost suffocated him in Kentucky.

After about an hour, an orange glow appeared to the south. Monroe ran his hands over his eyes, wiping away the sleep that threatened and the weariness that had overtaken his body. When he opened them again, the glow remained.

Puzzled, he resisted the urge to nudge Pender to go faster. A terrible suspicion crept into his mind.

Impatient, he rode out the remaining miles, the glow intensifying the closer he got, until he was perhaps only a mile away.

Then it became horribly clear.

Flames rose from the roof of his beautiful, nearly finished hotel.

Monroe fought the urge to vomit, and instead pushed the horse faster. Everything he'd worked for, bled for, pushed his body so hard for over the last few months was burning.

His poor horse could not move fast enough. "Sorry, boy." He leaned forward—anything to close the distance between himself and the fire, and Emma. "I'll give you the best brushing down of your life later. And all the apples you can eat. Just get me there before it's all gone."

Monroe could swear the flames leapt higher the closer he got. Had Emma arrived yet? He could hardly imagine her reaction to the fire. She had so loved the building. The most vivid memory of her jumped into his mind. With awe in her eyes, she'd run her fingers over the woodworking around the powder-room door before she'd been locked in. Fierce pride had risen inside him. It was almost as if she'd been touching him.

He was still a half mile out when he felt the heat. It was a gradual rise in temperature from the already hot night. A quarter of a mile away, he could make out the people. A line of them, stretching around the burning hotel and disappearing into the darkness toward the wagon path that led to the creek.

And the roar. The fire sounded downright angry.

Heat seared his face as he rode up. Monroe reined Pender back, pulling him away from the line and around to the front of the building. The men, some only half-dressed, passed buckets up and down the line—a bucket brigade.

Monroe jumped off his exhausted horse. "You, Carter!" He grabbed a tall, lean boy from the line. Carter had been his youngest hire, straight off the dirt streets of Denver and hoping for more than an existence holding up a barstool like his daddy. "Take Pender to the stable. Brush him down real good and make sure he's got plenty of feed and water."

"Yes, sir, Mr. Hartley." The boy took the reins from Monroe. "I'm awful sorry about your hotel."

"Save the sorry for later." Monroe clapped him on the back and ran toward the front of the line. Someone was shouting orders—a female voice. Mrs. Ruby, perhaps. He couldn't imagine the quieter Mrs. McFarland taking charge of a group of men this way. Smoke and exertion made the woman's voice crack.

The heat of the fire warmed the side of his face as he searched for the person connected to the voice. It wasn't only men working to save the hotel, but Emma's friends—the other Gilbert Girls—were all up near the front of the line. Hair coming loose from the braids down their backs and robes knotted over their nightshifts, the girls worked just as fast as his men. He scanned their faces for Emma, but she wasn't there. She had to be somewhere nearby.

A sweaty, red-faced McFarland, hastily clad in rumpled pants and suspenders over his long johns, directed new arrivals from the camp to the creek. It took a moment before he recognized Monroe.

"What happened?" Monroe demanded, raising his voice in order to be heard over the fire. He shielded his eyes from the scorching flames, not just because of the heat but because he didn't want to know what had already been destroyed. All he wanted to know was what he could save.

McFarland squinted at Monroe and shook his head, his only reaction to Monroe's sudden appearance. "Not certain." He turned to two men who'd just run up from the tent camp. "To the creek, boys. We're starting another line." He pointed the newcomers, their faces wide awake despite the late hour, toward the trees. "I don't know why you're here, but you picked a good time to return."

Monroe almost smiled. It wasn't much of a greeting, but it was better than when he'd left. "Where's Turner?"

"Haven't seen him. Haven't had a moment to look for him."

"Who's up front, barking orders?"

McFarland smirked. "Someone else who couldn't stay away. Get on up there. We need to get this out before the whole thing's gutted."

Monroe didn't waste another second. Weaving around McFarland and the men at the head of the line who tossed bucket after bucket of water onto the fire, he blinked to clear his vision.

"We need a ladder. No, we need several ladders. At least four or five. You there, can you get them? Take a few men with you. It's imperative we get to the second floor." The woman's voice cracked again, and she coughed a little.

That voice . . .

There! Monroe spotted her as four men raced past him toward the camp, presumably for the ladders she'd requested.

"Emma?" Monroe whispered the name to himself. He took a few steps forward. It *was* her. Her tan and maroon dress drooped strangely around her legs, and her hair had come loose from where some of it was still pinned up. She wore no hat and no gloves. She looked wild. And determined.

Determined to save his hotel.

The second he'd woken from the night he spent slumped on the lobby floor, he knew he was in love with her. But that feeling paled in comparison to what coursed through him now.

It was nothing he'd felt before. It was love, but something even more. He couldn't describe it. It had been different with Colette. She'd needed protecting outside the world of her family's ranch. Even though he wanted to protect Emma, she was no wilting flower. Instead, she stood with her hands on her hips, orange flames framing the fierce look on her face as she not only fought to save his hotel, but organized everyone else to save it too.

His strong, independent woman. And he'd let her down. Turned her away. Rejected her. Shame flooded him, and he had to force it from his mind. There would be time aplenty to deal with that later.

"I need someone to organize the men around back!" Emma yelled.

"I'll do it." Monroe crossed the space between them, the prickly grass crunching under his feet, although he couldn't hear it over the roar of the flames.

"Monroe." Her breath caught as she swayed a little. "I . . . I came back . . ."

He quickly grasped her hand. "Later. We'll have all the time in the world then."

She smiled at him, her face streaked with sweat and soot. He let go and reached for a bucket near her feet. "Let's save this hotel."

He turned then and forced himself to look at everything he'd done over the past few months, eaten alive by a living, breathing monster. He needed to concentrate on the task at hand or else he'd take Emma into his arms and prove to her how sorry he was, right here in front of everyone, while his life's work burned to the ground behind them.

Gripping the handle between his hands, he let himself take one last look back at Emma. She stared after him, her mouth agape, until a group of men ran up with the ladders she'd asked for. He could swear he caught the hint of lemons even with all the smoke in the air.

He'd underestimated her. He could scarcely believe he was only figuring that out now. Their future was never his decision.

It was hers.

The fire almost growled as something collapsed inside the entry. It jolted him into action, and he raced around the south end of the building.

At least twenty men had begun forming a line behind the hotel. At the head, with a full bucket, was an older, grizzled fellow who normally preferred the bottle to work. But every time Monroe was set to let him go, the man had proved himself in some extraordinary way—noticing when measurements were just a little off, or when someone else had missed a finishing touch that would have been glaringly obvious in the final product.

"Aim for the dining room!" Monroe shouted to him and the other man with buckets at the head of the line. If they moved from right to left—from the dining room toward the middle of the hotel—perhaps he could prevent the fire from restarting where they'd already put it out. He hurried down the row of men. "Move those buckets! The faster we douse it, the quicker it'll go out."

After checking that the men at the creek had sufficient buckets and leaving the one he'd brought with them, he ran back to the front of the line. Adrenaline kept him moving, despite an entire day spent in the saddle.

"Right there!" He pointed to where flames licked the furthest dining room window. Someone had already shattered the glass in order to toss water inside. Monroe moved closer. He put up an arm to shield his face. Inch by inch, he stepped nearer to his life's greatest work. All he wanted was to see inside. To see what remained intact. The chair rail along the wall, perhaps, or the beautiful buffet table they'd so carefully placed near the side of the room, the ornate tables and chairs that had been due to arrive just a few days ago, or the crown molding on the ceiling.

It was no use. The heat singed the hairs on his arms. A lick of flame burst from the window, sending him careening back, but not before it swept across his shirt. Monroe beat at his chest with both hands, putting out the embers that clung to the fabric.

Bucket after bucket, the men at the head of the line tossed water through the open window. Finally, the flames diminished in this one corner of the building. Monroe wasn't certain how much time had passed. It could have been minutes, or it could have been an hour. Flames still raged throughout the hotel.

"Move to the next window," Monroe shouted.

The men obliged. Monroe kept them at a steady pace between the hotel and the creek, ensuring the buckets moved as quickly as possible.

They put out the fire in the rear of the dining room, only as flames burst even more heavily from the second floor.

"More ladders!" Monroe yelled to the men in the middle of the line. They ran, and he took their places, passing full buckets up the line and empty ones back down, as they tried to douse the fire that remained in the rear of the hotel's first floor.

In between passes, Monroe tilted his head back and wiped at his burning eyes. While much of the downstairs was now dark and smoking, the second floor still burned.

It was useless.

No.

He couldn't give in. Not yet. Not while he was still standing. Not while these men fought. Not while Emma stood her ground up front. The men arrived with the ladders and leaned them up wherever it looked safe enough.

"Here." The man behind him nudged his arm with a full bucket.

Monroe took it and passed it on.

A drop of water in an ocean of flame.

Chapter Thirty-three

S weat dripped its way down Emma's face, down her back, down her front. Never had she been so hot, filthy, or disheveled.

Never had she felt so alive.

Except, she had to admit to herself, when she was with Monroe. But this was different. While spending time with him was exhilarating—heart-pounding, shaky hands, words that tumbled from her mouth at a rate her brain could barely process—and yet so comfortable too, this made her feel . . . strong. Capable. She was fighting a fire, and she was determined to win.

Hands on her hips, she surveyed the line of men and women in front of her. They'd been working nonstop for nearly two hours, when she'd ridden up on that old work horse and had spotted the flames spewing from the first floor. Racing to the camp, she'd yelled until the men came stumbling from their tents. Now, finally, the fire had grown smaller. Thick smoke wafted up from the first floor, making the men on the ladders that were spread across the front of the hotel cough. Most had pulled handkerchiefs over their mouths and noses, but the smoke still snuck through.

"We're almost there," she shouted to the line. "Not too much longer now."

"We'll do this all night if we have to," Penny replied, her voice as thick and cracked as Emma's own.

A fierce pride shot through Emma as she watched Penny and the other girls pass the buckets back and forth. Clad in nightclothes—items they normally would have never dared wear in front of men—the girls hadn't even hesitated when Emma had run to the house and asked them to join in. Even Millie had joined the group, although she'd held back at first, her eyes wide with fright as she'd taken in the flames.

"What are you doing?"

Emma twisted around, searching for the angry voice. She didn't have to look long.

Mr. Turner burst through the smoke, his face hard. He grabbed her by the arm and pulled her away from the line. "This is *my* hotel. I demand to know what you're doing."

Emma tried to yank her arm away, but he held firm. "I'm saving it, obviously. And it isn't *your* hotel." She wanted to spit in his face, but her throat was so dry that her words would have to suffice.

"It is, now that your *suitor* is gone. As such, I'm in charge of this operation."

"Then where have you been? The fire's been burning for hours!" Emma winced as his fingers dug harder into her arm.

"That ain't your business. I'm taking charge now." With that, he let her go and marched back toward the line.

Emma ran after him, her legs jelly but somehow still holding her up.

"Get down off those ladders! Everyone stand back. Put the buckets down," he ordered as he yanked a full bucket from Millie's hands. He stared at her for a moment, then shook his head. "Worthless," he muttered.

Emma didn't have time to wonder after that remark. What was he doing? If they stopped now, the fire could roar back to life and burn the entire structure to the ground. "But we've made such progress," she said. "We can't stop now."

"They can and they will." He looked out over the line, where people stood silent, buckets in their hands. "The best course is to let this fire burn itself out."

"No!" Emma ran in front of him. "We need to keep moving. If we give up now, it'll come back and take the whole building."

Turner glared at her, then turned to the crowd. "I'm the boss of this operation, not this woman. I demand you disperse. Now."

Emma held his gaze. She was *not* giving up. Not after how hard they'd all worked to put the fire out. And not for this man, of all people. "They will not." She paused, narrowing her eyes as she searched his face. The way he shifted and looked at the hotel, his insistence that everyone stop working . . . there was something odd about it all. "Why, you want the hotel to burn, don't you?"

"You need to shut your mouth. Or else . . ."

He gripped her arm again, harder this time. Emma bit her lip so as not to give him the satisfaction of seeing her wince. "What are you planning to do?

Hold me at gunpoint again?" She kept her voice low, the words seething from her mouth.

"If that's what it takes," he said, pulling her away from the line and into the smoke.

Emma tugged at her arm, but it was useless.

"You let her go!" a voice shouted through the smoke. Millie appeared, her red hair nearly loose and her face streaked with soot.

Emma barely had time to register Millie's presence before Turner yanked her even farther into the smoke. Her heart fought wildly and her eyes searched for Millie or anyone else, but the gray haze was too dense. She could barely even see Turner.

He pulled her around to what she thought was the side of the hotel, but perhaps it was down toward the tracks. No, it couldn't be, or the smoke would have dissipated. It was impossible to tell exactly where they were at all.

"You won't destroy everything I've earned, Miss Daniels." His words were like the smoke that floated around them, wrapping their way around her mind and her body and suffocating her. "I've worked too hard to get this hotel, and I'm not going to let Hartley's little woman take it from me."

Emma opened her mouth to speak, but the smoke was too much and she fell into a coughing fit instead.

"Now you're quiet. I like you better that way." His face appeared through the smoke that clouded her vision and stung her eyes. "You say too much. You *know* too much."

She pushed away from him, but he gripped her arm even tighter and twisted it behind her. Her throat closed up. "All I know is that you want the hotel to burn." The words stung her throat and she coughed again.

"And you don't have the good sense to keep it to yourself. So let's take this down to the creek, away from all of these people, shall we?" His tone was eerily conversational.

She stumbled a bit as he pushed her forward. What was he planning to do? She didn't wish to find out. Emma opened her mouth to scream or shout for help or say anything at all, but her voice was gone again. All that came out was a ragged, sad little sound following by more coughing.

"Cat got your tongue?" He laughed and it sent prickles up her spine. "Now move."

He pushed her forward again, and her feet had no choice but to comply. She had to keep her wits about her, since it seemed her voice had abandoned her already. A way out, that was what she needed. But how?

She tried to keep a slow pace so she could have more time to think of a solution, but he kept pushing her harder. A pain shot through her twisted arm, and she gritted her teeth together.

"It'll be such a sad accident," he said, almost cheerfully. "Poor Miss Daniels returned to Crest Stone and bravely tried to save her lover's work, only to find herself lost in the smoke. How was she to know where the creek was in all of this haze?"

Bile rose from Emma's stomach. He was planning to murder her. For what? To see Monroe's work destroyed? There had to be more to it. But she couldn't think about that now. She had to get away, somehow. She could turn and hit him with her free hand. Except he'd figure out what she was doing before she could get all the way around. And she couldn't give him notice, or he'd have time to pull his gun. If only she had a rock or something else hard that she could hit him with first. If she couldn't use her hands, then what else did she have?

Her feet.

She could try to pull away and run, but his grip was too strong. She could trip on purpose and slow them both down, and then perhaps she could kick him.

That was it. Her only choice. Her one chance at surviving this. She had to take it.

Emma pushed her lips together and sent up a quick prayer even as her heart quickened. It had to work. She took a deep breath, stumbled over her own feet, and fell to the ground.

"Get up," Turner growled at her.

But as she rose, she drew her right foot forward and then sent it backward as hard as she could.

Turner grunted. His grip on her arm slackened a little bit, just enough for her to turn around and raise her foot again. But before she could kick him, he redoubled his hold and pulled her to the ground. Emma fought, but it was not enough.

Turner raised his hand and Emma closed her eyes, braced for the impact. But it never came.

Instead, she heard him curse. Then there was a shuffling sound almost drowned out by the noise of the remaining fire. Turner's hand left her shoulder. She opened her eyes and looked up.

And there, right next to her, Monroe had Turner pinned to the ground. In a split second, Turner landed his fist into Monroe's face. Emma scrambled to her feet and looked around wildly for something to use to end the fight.

Monroe didn't budge. Turner struck him again, and this time, Monroe's strength gave just enough that Turner gained the upper hand. He flipped Monroe over, but it lasted for only a few seconds. Monroe's fist found Turner's stomach, and the man coiled into himself, allowing Monroe to struggle to his feet.

Emma took a step backward, still casting her eyes across the ground. She took another step back—right into a person.

"Emma!" Caroline said. "We saw you get dragged off. Millie ran to find Monroe while we came to search for you." Dora and Penny flanked Caroline. They were all ashamble, and Emma had never been so glad to see them in her life. She flung herself into Penny's arms while Caroline rested a hand on Emma's back.

A grunt pulled her attention to the men again. Turner drew his hand away from Monroe's face, but in no time, Monroe pinned him to the ground again. This time, Turner stayed put. After a moment, Monroe hauled him up. Holding both Turner's arms behind the man's back, Monroe cast his eyes toward Emma. She ran gratefully to him.

"Are you all right?" he asked, his face drawn as he searched her with his eyes.

She nodded. In the haze and the darkness, it was impossible to see what damage Turner might have done to Monroe's face. She lifted a hand and let her fingers caress his cheek, just as she'd dreamed of doing a hundred times. He smiled at her, a shadow of that old teasing grin lurking beneath the exhaustion, before turning back to Turner with a grimace. "Let's go." With that, he pushed Turner toward the front of the hotel.

"Where?" Turner spat, as Emma and the other girls hurried to keep up with them.

"To see McFarland."

Turner said no more, and Emma imagined he was dreaming up all manner of falsehoods to spew upon arrival. Monroe led the way directly through the smoke, somehow knowing exactly which direction to go. Millie appeared, seemingly out of nowhere. If what Caroline said was true, Emma owed her life to this girl who had betrayed her not a week earlier. Emma reached for her hand, and Millie hesitated before taking it.

"Thank you," Emma said.

Millie said not a word, but looked up at Emma and smiled.

The bucket brigade was still working when they arrived at the hotel, and the fire had been reduced to a mere nuisance in the northeast corner of the second floor.

"McFarland!" Monroe bellowed the moment the man was in hearing distance.

Several faces turned their way, smoke-reddened eyes wide at the sight of Monroe holding Turner by his collar, his hands wrenched behind his back. McFarland appeared from the front of the line, rubbing a soot-covered hand across his face.

"What is this?" he said as he drew closer.

"A misunderstanding," Turner replied, his voice smooth as if he'd simply been on a stroll across the valley.

Monroe pushed him away. Turner pulled on the collar of his shirt and glowered at him.

"A misunderstanding in which you were trying to harm Miss Daniels?" Monroe spat at him.

"We were simply having a conversation," Turner replied. He looked right at Emma, and her stomach turned.

No one could possibly believe his word over theirs this time.

Chapter Thirty-four

The man's words made Monroe's fingers itch. He balled them into fists, ready to land them on Turner's face again. But how were he and Emma going to convince McFarland of anything at this point? He opened his mouth to speak, but before he could, Emma's brash friend—Miss May—stepped forward.

"It was no such thing." Miss May held her finger a mere inch from Turner's chest. "Everyone here saw you drag her off."

"I did not," Turner said in a measured voice. "This woman is hysterical."

"She sounds perfectly reasonable to me." Monroe glared at the man. How he'd ever felt any empathy for Turner, he had no idea.

"You'd gone to the rear to check the progress of the men working there," Emma said to McFarland.

"She speaks the truth," Miss Sinclair said, quietly. She almost shrank into herself as she spoke.

Everyone turned to look at Miss Sinclair, including McFarland, whose considerable brows knitted together. The other girls moved closer to her, almost protectively. Monroe was just thankful that Miss Sinclair had finally seen Turner for the rat he was.

"You can't believe the word of these . . . these so-called *ladies* over mine, sir," Turner sputtered as he sneered at Miss Sinclair.

His words made Monroe's fists clench again. How he'd love to see this man get the justice he sorely deserved.

McFarland looked Turner up and down, almost certainly taking in the white of his shirt—streaked only with dirt, not soot—and his clean face. The signs of a man who had not been working to extinguish the fire. "Where were you all evening?"

"Asleep. I knew nothing of this fire until just a few minutes ago."

McFarland stroked his chin. He had to see through those lies. Monroe didn't know where Turner had been, but he doubted he'd slept through all this chaos. No one could have.

Anger boiled up through Monroe again. What this man had almost done to Emma. What he'd already done to them both. His hotel in flames. He could no longer stay quiet. "What he *clearly* had was ill intentions toward Miss Daniels." The words ground their way through Monroe's teeth.

"He had no interest in putting out the fire," Miss May added. "In fact, he ordered us all to stop!"

"The fire was going to burn itself out. It was a waste of manpower trying to douse it," Turner said, his arms crossed.

Monroe scoffed. "That's why it's close to extinguished now."

"It's my hotel. I'm the one who should've taken charge," Turner growled, taking a step forward.

Monroe's entire body felt as if it had caught fire too. He looked Turner right in his eyes. "Under *no* circumstances is this your hotel."

McFarland held up his hands, but before he could speak, Miss Sinclair moved between Monroe and Turner.

"Have you something to add, Miss Sinclair?" McFarland asked.

She twisted her hands together, then glanced at Turner, who narrowed his eyes at her. Emma moved toward her and slid an arm through Miss Sinclair's. That one simple gesture nearly melted Monroe's heart. Who else was so kind and forgiving as to take the arm of the woman who'd ruined her position here?

"Then speak up." McFarland's mustache twitched as he glanced toward the hotel. Not much remained of the fire, but it was enough that the men had to keep on it, or else it would roar back to life.

"He started the fire," Miss Sinclair said in a small voice, her eyes fixed on McFarland.

Monroe went cold.

"That's preposterous!" Turner boomed. "She only wants to see me brought down because she threw herself at me like some kind of loose woman, and she's angry that I refused her."

McFarland held up a hand to indicate he should shut his mouth, as Miss Sinclair gasped, shaking her head.

Could it be true that Turner started the fire? Monroe watched Turner for any sign, but the man was as rigid as a tree and showed no emotion beyond outrage. But Emma . . . Her eyes widened just a bit, almost as if something finally made sense for her. Monroe forced himself to breathe.

"That's quite a serious charge. What makes you think that, Miss Sinclair?" McFarland asked.

"He . . . he mentioned once, a week or so back, before Emma and Mr. Hartley were let go, that he'd like to burn the place to the ground." Her voice gained power the more she spoke, almost as if she were exacting her own revenge for the way Turner had used her.

Turner threw up his hands. "You can't believe a word she says."

"You'd best keep quiet and let her speak." Monroe kept his words level, not betraying the rage that threatened to burst through. If what Miss Sinclair said was true—and he suspected it was—it was going to take every man here to keep him off Turner. It explained why Turner was nowhere to be found while they were all working so hard to put the fire out. He conveniently appeared when it seemed they would be successful.

"Go on," McFarland said to Miss Sinclair. "Why'd he say such a thing?"

"Because it was almost finished. He wanted to build it from scratch under his charge. He'd be paid more as the builder, and it would be his rather than a project that was really someone else's. If . . . " She swallowed hard. "If you look in his tent, I imagine you'll find a quantity of empty whiskey bottles."

At that, Turner lunged for Miss Sinclair. She froze as his hand clamped around her arm.

Emma held fast to her other arm and pounded at Turner's hand. "Let her go, you . . . you . . ."

It was as if she couldn't think of a word vile enough for the man. Monroe leapt forward at the same moment McFarland wrapped his arms around Turner. It only took one good shot to Turner's gut to make him release the girl. Emma pulled her back toward the other ladies as McFarland wrestled Turner to the ground.

"Quick," Monroe shouted to the girls. "Get some rope."

Miss May ran for the barn.

He turned to the man on the ground and spat. "You're lucky it's not me that's got you down there. You're done, you hear me? You'll never so much as look at Miss Sinclair or Miss Daniels again, never mind put their lives in danger."

Turner sputtered something, but it was drowned out by McFarland's command to keep quiet.

Miss May was back quickly with an armful of rope. Together, McFarland and Monroe lashed Turner's hands together behind his back.

"I'll take him down to my place and then send someone to retrieve the bottles in his tent. We can ride for the sheriff in the morning. Why don't you get back to saving your hotel?" McFarland heaved Turner forward, down toward the tracks, leaving Monroe standing, his chest heaving, as he watched them disappear.

His hotel. He dared not hope.

"You heard what he said, girls." Emma's voice, ragged but determined, rang out behind him. "Let's save this hotel!"

With renewed vigor, Emma's friends rejoined the line. Emma wrapped an arm around Miss Sinclair's shoulders and said something that made the girl smile before she let go and the girl raced to join the others. As Emma went to follow them, Monroe reached for her hand. It was small and warm in his own, but he also knew it was strong. He drew her toward him until she was but a breath away.

"Thank you," was all he said. It summed up everything in his heart—her effort to put out the fire, her trust in him before he broke it, her return to find him, her kindness toward Miss Sinclair.

"I should be the one thanking you," she said. "You found me when I thought for certain he would . . ."

Her breath was warm on his face. He wanted so badly to kiss her, to wipe away all that had happened since Turner had found them by the creek. But he wouldn't, not until he'd asked her what he should have last week.

"Emma? May I ask you a question?"

Chapter Thirty-five

Her breath caught in her throat. The way Monroe was looking at her, his dark eyes intent on her own, nearly melted her in the heat of the remaining fire. It felt as if months had passed since they'd last stood like this, rather than merely a week.

"Yes?" she said, almost hesitantly. Her voice scraped against her throat, raw from shouting and smoke.

He fell to one knee, still holding her hands. She swallowed hard.

"I made the biggest mistake of my life last week." He kept his eyes pinned on hers. She couldn't look away even if she'd wanted to. "Instead of asking what *you* wanted, I assumed I already knew. That was wrong. You aren't like any other woman, and I shouldn't have made that decision for you. I've come to realize that it doesn't matter to me where I am or what I'm doing, so long as you're with me. If I have you, I can be happy anywhere. So now, I'll ask you. I love you and I want you to marry me, Emma Daniels."

Emma's chest bloomed with warmth. Emotion threatened to choke her, and it took everything she had not to let the tears stream from her eyes. How badly she'd wanted him to say those words that last day at the house. And now, here he was, finally asking for her. Except, he hadn't *actually* asked . . .

"But," he continued, "I need to know what you want. Do you want to live the life of a builder's wife, moving from place to place every few months? Or would you prefer to settle into a fixed home in a town somewhere? If you want land, we could start a small ranch. If you'll have me, that is," he added quickly.

Emma opened her mouth, but before she could speak, he dropped one of her hands and held up a finger.

"Before you answer, know that your decision—whatever it may be—is perfect for me. I'll do what you want to do."

Emma's mouth fell open. "You mean you'd give up the career you've worked so hard for . . . for me?"

"Yes," he said, his face perfectly serious, "I will, if that's what you choose. And you will never hear a word of complaint from me."

Her heart dipped. He was willing to give up his life's dream, all for her. Tears pricked at her eyes again, and she blinked them away rapidly. "Monroe, I would never do such a thing. I love you. So yes, I will marry you, and yes, I will follow you anywhere. I want to see everything you can build. I want to see every corner of this country with you."

She could swear his face pinched just a little, almost as if the emotion were too much for him to handle. He hesitated, still kneeling. "Are you certain?"

"I've never been so certain of anything in my life," she whispered. "I came to realize that when I returned home."

He swallowed visibly. "I . . . My first wife, Colette. I told you that she died." He paused again, almost as if he was struggling with the words. "What I didn't say—what I've never said to anyone—is how it was my fault." He looked at her intently, almost frantically.

"I don't understand," Emma said. "How could it be your fault?"

Anguish creased his brow as he held tightly to her hands. "You should know I would never wish the same to happen to you, so if you change your mind, I understand."

"Monroe." Emma sunk to the ground herself, her hands still in his. She was thankful the smoke mostly obscured them from view. "Tell me. Please."

He kept haunted eyes on her as he spoke. "Soon after Colette and I were married, I found the work of my dreams. A nearby rancher had seen what I'd done with the outbuildings at Colette's family's ranch. He asked me to build a new home for his family. I agreed, and Colette and I moved there so I could complete that project. Not long after that, a visiting friend of his asked me to build him a home back in Denver, so we then lived in the city for a few months. It kept on like that, following jobs wherever they took us. Denver, mining camps, railroad towns, Pueblo, Colorado Springs, ranches. It was my dream. But it wasn't Colette's. She missed her family, missed the friends she'd made when we lived briefly in Denver, and she hated the mining camps and railroad towns."

He took a deep breath, and Emma squeezed his hands, letting him know she was still there, still listening.

"She became more and more withdrawn," he continued. "She lost color and stayed in bed all day. I didn't know what to do. I spent as much time with her as I could, but she had no female companionship in those places. We were in a mining town in the mountains when she took ill with a fever. It wasn't long before the fever took her."

The anguish on his face was too much for Emma. "That wasn't your fault."

"It was," he said in a choked voice. "She was my responsibility. I knew it was wearing her down, and yet I kept dragging her from place to place."

Emma pulled her hands from his and placed them on each side of his face. "It was *not* your fault."

He gripped her arms, his face torn with memories and grief that hadn't been spoken until now.

"Yes, she was sad," Emma said. "She was lonely. But that fever was not something you could have prevented. It could've happened anywhere, at any time."

He said nothing for a moment, only watched her as he wrestled with his emotions. "I'm sorry I didn't ask you at the house, in front of everyone. All I could think of was how my life might kill you too. I couldn't do that to you. I couldn't force you into that situation." His fingers held tighter to her arms. "It was only after you'd left that I realized how stupid I'd been. That I should've told you everything and let you make the decision."

His words went straight to her heart, repairing all the hurt that lingered there. "My answer is yes. Yes to you. Yes to everything. What makes you happy makes me happy too."

He dropped his hands and crushed her into his arms. "Are you certain?" he whispered into her hair.

"I am. Completely." She relaxed there in his embrace. This was home, in his arms, no matter where they were. "But Monroe . . ." There was still one rather large problem. One that could turn all of this into just a dream. She pushed away, creating some space between them.

"What is it?" he asked.

"I still have to support my family. They're desperate. My sisters have found work in a factory, but it's awful. Dirty, crowded, loud, and they're trapped in there all day from sunrise to sundown. And the pay still isn't enough to cover

Mama's doctor expenses if she should fall ill again. I need to find some kind of work to support them. I'm the eldest. They are my responsibility." She frowned again. How could she find work if they kept moving around? And would there be reputable work for a married woman in the places they'd be?

He placed both her hands between his. "Your family will be my family. And I don't let my family go without. The money I'd make from building is more than we could ever use together. I'd be honored to send some of that sum to your mother, especially since I can't send any to my own."

Emma wasn't certain she'd heard him correctly. "But you don't even know them."

He shook his head. "It does not matter. Besides, I met one of your sisters briefly when I went looking for you in Louisville. She was a delight." He chuckled.

"You came looking for me?" She'd had no idea. Lily must've taken him to task when he met her.

"I did. It's a beautiful city, though awfully hot. I saw quite a bit of it trying to find you."

Emma had to force her mouth closed. Then she shook her head. "I can't let you do that. It's my burden, not yours."

He raised his hands to her face, placing one gently on each of her cheeks. "You don't understand. If we're to be married, your burdens become mine too. And your family certainly isn't a burden."

Something inside Emma shattered. She clung to his arms to keep herself from collapsing to the ground as relief coursed through her. All that fear, all that guilt at her sisters having to work, it all burst into pieces at his words. She no longer had to carry all of that alone. "Thank you," was all she could think to say.

He pulled her to him. "I'd do anything to make you happy." He whispered the words in her ear as he stroked her tangled hair.

She leaned into him. "We should get back to the fire."

"After I do this." He took her face in his hands again and raised it to meet his.

Emma's entire body shook with the emotion of that kiss. For so long, she'd imagined his lips on hers. It was perfect. Monroe was hers, and she would get to see all of this land with him by her side. Her family would want for nothing. Everything was going to be fine.

"Hello, my lovebirds! We have a fire here." Penny's voice broke through the haze Emma floated in. She was standing over them.

Monroe laughed. He kissed Emma again and then dropped his hands. "You heard the lady."

Emma smiled up at him. She couldn't wait to spend the rest of her life with him, wherever that life might take them.

Epilogue

Emma wore a simple light blue skirt topped with a matching blue bodice that, to her, resembled the color of the Colorado sky. Her friends in Crest Stone had bought her a lovely seed pearl necklace that now rested around her neck, and Caroline had lent her a blue hat. Emma ran her gloved hands over the ensemble. She had never seen a more perfect dress or a more beautiful necklace, even compared to the expensive silk gowns and jewelry some of her friends back home had worn for their weddings.

She'd also never seen a more perfect setting. Even the soaring St. Martin of Tours church at home had nothing on the bright yellow sun in this expansive cloudless sky, the mountains standing watch on either side of the valley, the golden asters and blue bellflowers, and closest to her heart—the partially re-built hotel behind her.

But most perfect of all were the people. The girls—Caroline, Dora, Penny, Millie, and the other newer girls—had become as close to her as her sisters at home. No matter where she went, she knew she'd remain friends with them for life. It was most wonderful to have them here since her own family had been unable to make the journey.

And Monroe. He stood before her now, clad in his finest clothing—a new gray suit with a string tie and a starched white shirt. His brown hair was freshly cut and combed perfectly down, and his boots shone in the sunlight. He stood waiting for her with Big Jim by his side and the preacher from Cañon City to the left. On the preacher's other side, Emma's friends waited, wearing the best dresses they'd brought from home. Penny winked at her, and Emma couldn't help grinning back.

"Ready?" Mr. McFarland whispered.

She nodded and he took her arm. He'd agreed without hesitation to walk her down the aisle. She almost burst at the fatherly pride he showed, particularly since he and Mrs. McFarland had married too late to have children of their own.

The "aisle" was but a path worn from feet making the walk to and from the tracks. Her guests were all men from the building crew, along with the newest Gilbert Girls who'd arrived in time for the hotel's original scheduled opening. Since it was delayed, they'd made do the best they could, some of them sleeping in tents provided by the building crew, who in turn slept outside, and serving guests sandwiches where they sat on the train. Mrs. Ruby and Mrs. McFarland had welcomed Emma back with open arms as a guest when they learned of Turner's scheme. While she wasn't allowed to officially work for the Gilbert Company any longer because she'd broken a cardinal rule, she'd wanted to help and the women had gladly let her. And when no one was looking, Mrs. McFarland did some creative bookkeeping and slipped Emma the wages she would have earned if she'd still been officially employed.

When they reached the preacher, Mr. McFarland stepped aside and Monroe took his place after they shook hands. After Monroe, Mr. McFarland, and a couple of men from the crew had delivered Turner to the sheriff in Cañon City, Monroe accepted Mr. McFarland's offer to resume his old role and lead the rebuilding of the hotel under an even tighter schedule. McFarland had kept his word and not informed Mr. Gilbert of the reason behind Monroe's termination, but McFarland insisted that Monroe use his mistake in courting Emma to lecture the crew on how not to act with the ladies at the house. Emma wasn't sure how much good that did, considering the young man who watched Caroline from the front row at the moment.

"Hello there, Miss Daniels," Monroe whispered to her as he took her hand.

"Hello, Mr. Hartley," she said, warmth snaking up her body again. She wondered if her reaction to him would ever subside. She hoped it wouldn't.

"Ladies and gentlemen," the preacher began. "We are gathered here for the joining of two of God's children in holy matrimony."

The ceremony passed too quickly, even as Emma tried to thoroughly live each moment of it. The way Monroe looked at her as he slipped the slim golden band around her finger. The pride in his eyes when the preacher pronounced them man and wife. The tender kiss he placed on her lips as one of the girls played a happy tune on the piano some of the men had carried up from the house earlier that day.

"Till forever," Monroe said, his forehead touching hers.

"Forever," she repeated. "And everywhere."

He kissed her again as the audience erupted in cheers.

Nothing could ever be more perfect.

THANK YOU FOR READING! Now you have to find out what happens next! Who's that man watching Caroline? And what is Caroline's secret? Her story is next, and you can get it here: http://bit.ly/RunningForeverBook

To find out when the next *Gilbert Girls* book is available, sign up here: http://bit.ly/catsnewsletter I also give subscribers a free *Gilbert Girls* prequel novella (it tells the story of Mr. and Mrs. McFarland), sneak peeks at upcoming books, insights into the writer life, discounts and deals, the opportunity to join my advance reader team, inspirations, and so much more. I'd love to have *you* join the fun!

Turn the page for a sneak peek at Caroline's story, *Running From Forever* . .
.

Books in *The Gilbert Girls* series
Building Forever[1]
Running From Forever[2]
Wild Forever[3]
Hidden Forever[4]
Forever Christmas[5]

1. http://bit.ly/BuildingForeverbook

2. http://bit.ly/RunningForeverBook

3. http://bit.ly/WildForeverBook

4. http://bit.ly/HiddenForeverBook

5. http://bit.ly/ForeverChristmasBook

Sneak peek at Running From Forever (The Gilbert Girls, Book Two)
Chapter One

Thomas Drexel was lucky.

Or at least he had been lately. He was lucky that Monroe Hartley had hired him back in Denver, when all he needed was to get out of town as fast as possible. He was lucky the work paid well. He was lucky no one much ever came to this hidden valley. And even when the hotel burned up all his hard work over the summer, he was lucky they needed to rebuild and kept him on.

He hoped his luck would hold now. It was either that or go to California or Mexico—someplace no one would ever think to look for him. He pulled off his hat, smoothed down his sun-streaked hair, and knocked on the door of the McFarlands' apartment.

Mrs. McFarland answered, rosy-cheeked and smiling as always.

"Ma'am, I work—or worked, really—on the building crew. I'm Thomas Drexel. I'm wondering if I might have a word with your husband?"

"You must be hungry," she said by way of inviting him in.

"No need to trouble yourself." He inched in, feeling six kinds of awkward in her well-kept home. Thomas hadn't seen the inside of it since he'd helped finish installing the wood trim a few weeks ago. As the hotel manager and the bookkeeper, Mr. and Mrs. McFarland were appointed a three-room apartment on the first floor of the hotel.

"Nonsense," Mrs. McFarland said with a warm smile. "Do sit. I'll fetch Mr. McFarland and some hot cakes and bacon."

Thomas' stomach rumbled at the very mention of bacon. The building crew usually made do with a stew of venison or rabbit and, if a man had enough time to make a trip to Canon City, some cheese or bread. It had been non-stop work since the hotel had burned in early August. Now, finally, it was all completed and due to open to guests tomorrow.

"Thomas!" McFarland entered the room. He had seemingly transformed overnight from a grizzled bear of a man who'd worked on everything from repairing the existing buildings across the tracks to fetching supplies in town to a man with slicked-back hair, neatly trimmed beard, and, of all things, a suit.

Thomas blinked for a moment, trying to sort out what he saw. "Good morning," he said a bit stiffly.

McFarland laughed. "Surprised how I cleaned up?" he asked in his Irish brogue.

"No, sir." Thomas recovered quickly. He had a large favor to ask, and insulting the man wasn't exactly the best way to begin.

Mrs. McFarland arrived at that moment with two plates of hot cakes and bacon and two mugs of steaming coffee. It was perfect timing, both for the potential awkwardness of the situation and for Thomas' stomach.

After they'd both eaten their share of breakfast and discussed the state of the new hotel, Mr. McFarland asked, "What brings you to see me? Aside from my wife's cooking, that is."

Thomas drew in a breath. "I'm hoping that after the crew is dismissed today, I might stay on. I could do any sort of work. Carpentry, as you know. I'm good with horses and livestock. I can repair just about anything. I can fetch necessities from town. Anything you might need."

"Can you cook?" Mr. McFarland asked.

Thomas nearly choked on his coffee. "I . . . well, I can learn. I'm a quick study."

McFarland laughed again. "I'm joking. We have enough kitchen boys." He set his coffee on the lovely hand-carved low table. "You've been a good worker, Thomas. I could certainly find something for you to do here, but I'm curious why. You could find better-paying work with the building boom up in Denver, especially now that you have experience."

Thomas wasn't prepared for this question, but he quickly formulated an answer. "I like this place, this hotel. I feel at home here." He hoped that was enough to avoid any more questions.

McFarland nodded. "I've been here a while myself, since the days of the railroad camp. There's something about this valley."

Thomas nodded, even though he wasn't certain he felt the same way. He just needed to stay here, out of sight, tucked away in this valley where no one knew who he was.

McFarland was watching him. "Of course, I was also sweet on this girl whose family had a small ranch a few miles away."

Thomas' thoughts instantly flicked to the pretty blonde girl he'd first noticed at Hartley's wedding a couple of months back. Since that time, he'd seen her now and then—fetching food from the springhouse at the creek behind the hotel, making her way across the railroad tracks and the hill that stood between the new hotel and the old white house where she'd been living with the other girls, laughing as she entered the rebuilt hotel for the first time. He swallowed. The last thing he needed was McFarland suspecting him of breaking the rules with one of the Gilbert Girls, especially when he'd never even done as much as spoken to her. The hotel's restaurant waitresses were strictly forbidden, if a man wanted to keep his position with the Gilbert Company. "There's no girl."

The man kept his eyes on Thomas a moment longer, then nodded. "All right. If you want, you can start right away. The head chef has already requested more shelving in the pantry. Speak to him and find out what he wants."

"Yes, sir. Thank you." Thomas shook McFarland's hand and made his way back through the hotel toward the kitchen.

The large hotel lobby was mostly empty, save for a couple of new men behind the front desk and a more travel-weary man in front of it.

"Sir, I don't know if we're allowed to post those," one of the new hotel employees said.

"Then I'll wait for your boss." The dusty man in front of the desk dropped the saddlebags from his shoulder to the floor. He must have traveled all night to get here so early.

Thomas slowed his pace, eyes fixed on the front doors of the hotel but ears trained on the conversation at the desk.

"Go on," the traveler said to the man behind the desk. "'Lest you prefer scofflaws and murderers roaming free."

Out of the corner of his eye, Thomas could see one of the desk clerks move quickly toward the wing that housed McFarland's apartment.

Scofflaws and murderers.

Thomas swallowed hard and yanked his hat down farther over his eyes before sliding out one of the imposing front doors into the sunlight.

His days here might be more numbered than he'd thought.

Chapter Two

Caroline Beauchamp surveyed the hotel's dining room for the millionth time that morning. She wanted to ensure each table was at least two feet away from its neighbors, the floor was spotless, and the tablecloths showed not a single wrinkle. Somehow it calmed her to do things such as this. Speaking of the tablecloths . . .

She pinched a corner of cloth and examined it a bit more closely. These would need to pressed again today. She'd be certain to let Mrs. Ruby know after the morning meeting. One by one, the other girls streamed into the dining room, some yawning, others almost bursting with excitement. Penny and Dora, two of Caroline's first friends upon arriving in Crest Stone, made their way through the newer girls.

"Can you believe it's nearly here?" Penny's eyes sparkled and her entire body hummed with an excitement Caroline could feel.

"What if we make a mistake?" Dora asked. She twisted her hands together.

Caroline took one of her hands. "You won't. You've been training for this for months now. And it isn't so different from bringing the guests sandwiches onboard the train." Since the hotel and restaurant had caught fire in early August, which had delayed its opening, Mrs. Ruby had decided it would be most efficient and welcoming to make sandwiches and deliver them onboard the train cars to the waiting passengers as they traveled south to Santa Fe and north to Canon City.

Dora shook her head. Dark tendrils of hair wisped around her smooth, olive-skinned face. "It's not the same. This is so much more . . . formal."

"Don't fret about it," Penny said. "You know what you're doing. Now these other ninnies, I'm not so sure . . ." She waved a hand at the larger group.

Caroline scanned their faces. She spotted Millie and the three girls she'd arrived with halfway through the summer. And then there was a sea of exactly twenty-three other girls, most of whom had come just before the fire. Since that time, the newer girls had been living in canvas tents, which the building crew had kindly vacated until the Gilbert Company had sent a shipment of canvas. Caroline and her friends were the lucky ones—they'd been able to remain in their rooms at the old house. But last week, all the girls had moved into their dormitories inside the finally completed hotel. There was only one girl missing from the group.

"I wish Emma were here," Dora said quietly.

"As do I," Caroline said. "But I wouldn't take her happiness from her."

"She's off having grand adventures." Penny's face nearly glowed, as if she wished she were in Emma's place.

"I don't know how adventurous the California desert is," Caroline said. Emma had arrived with the three of them in late May, making their foursome the first Gilbert Girls in Crest Stone. But she had since married Monroe Hartley, the hotel's builder, and after staying to oversee the reconstruction of the Crest Stone Hotel, they had moved on just a couple of days ago to build another Gilbert Company hotel in California.

"Oh, but it is," Penny said. "Just think! Snakes, outlaws, scorpions, no water for miles and miles."

"That sounds horrifying," Caroline replied.

Dora nodded in agreement.

"You wouldn't know adventure if it knocked you in the head, Caroline Beauchamp. Why—" Penny's words stopped when Mrs. Ruby walked into the room.

"Good morning, ladies." Mrs. Ruby's voice boomed across the large room. "This is a day of last-minute preparations. I want you all to inspect your clothing, check your stations, and ensure the tables are spotless. Now that the hotel will be opening, twice-daily trains will begin stopping tomorrow at noon and six p.m. If you feel the need to practice serving today, then by all means, please do so.

"Please note that I'll be observing all of you over the next few days to select a head waitress and an assistant head waitress. In those positions, you will be privy to all decisions made regarding the dining room, you will be consulted regarding the hiring of new girls, you'll be in charge of the dining room when I am not present, and—of course—your pay will reflect your new role. You are dismissed."

The girls immediately began chattering among themselves as they broke off to attend their duties.

"Excuse me," Caroline said to her friends, who were already talking about who they thought could be named head waitress and assistant head waitress.

Mrs. Ruby was just finishing up answering a question for one of the newer girls when Caroline approached her. "Miss Beauchamp?"

"Mrs. Ruby, I was examining the tablecloths before you came in, and I believe they may need to be pressed again. They seem to have acquired a fair amount of wrinkles." Caroline reached for the nearest cloth and held up the end to show Mrs. Ruby.

The older woman squinted at the material and nodded. "Excellent work. The housemaids will need to press those before morning. I'll alert them." She paused and looked Caroline from head to toe before nodding in satisfaction. "I trust you were paying attention to my announcement?"

Caroline nodded. "Yes, ma'am."

"You have continued to prove yourself worthy of the Gilbert name. I see a great future for you in this company." With that, Mrs. Ruby moved faster than one would suspect a woman of her size could toward a group of girls congregated near the door to the kitchen.

Caroline's entire face went warm. Could Mrs. Ruby have been suggesting Caroline might be named head waitress? The thought made her arms and legs feel almost too light to work. Never had she thought she would come this far. When she'd arrived here in May from Boston, she'd felt like a tiny, timid mouse about to be buried under the sheer *emptiness* of this wild place. Everything had frightened her—Mrs. Ruby, the men building the hotel, the miners a few miles east, the sharpness of the mountains to the west, the way the sky seemed to go on and on, the lack of any comfort she'd had in the city. More than once, she had determined to resign herself to what awaited her if she returned to Boston, because at least that was familiar, even if it was what she'd run away from.

But she'd been lucky to make quick friends here. Penny, Dora, and Emma didn't know why she'd left Boston without telling a soul. What they did see was a girl who was capable of living up to the work expected from a Gilbert Girl. With their encouragement, Caroline worked and worked and worked, until she'd become proficient at chores she never would have even contemplated at home.

A smile tugged at the corner of her mouth as she wondered what her delicate older sister and her prim mother would say if they knew she could serve a table in under thirty minutes or wash her own clothing or—even worse—start a roaring fire to stay warm. That latest skill was newer, now that the nights had turned particularly chilly. Even the days had grown cool enough to require a coat on occasion. Snow had already come to the mountains above them, and according to Mrs. McFarland, it wouldn't be long until snow found its way to the valley.

Caroline didn't mind snow. She had learned she didn't mind hard work either. She felt useful here, unlike at home. There, she'd often imagined herself a prized sow to be trotted out at dinners and parties to eligible young men. Here, at Crest Stone, in this little valley surrounded by friends, she felt . . . *alive*. Free. Capable of providing for herself. Able to make her own decisions. She would never give that up.

All she had to do was remain hidden here.

Chapter Three

Thomas bit down on the nail between his teeth as he lined up the notches he'd cut in the two pieces of wood. If he was honest, he'd admit he'd never made shelving before. But surely it couldn't be that hard. After all, he'd helped build a hotel—twice.

The notches didn't line up. He spat the nail at the workbench he'd drug out of the shed behind the hotel. He needed a break before his annoyance boiled over into anger.

Although if he were being completely honest, it wasn't just the shelving that was fouling his mood. It was the man from earlier, the one with the wanted posters.

Thomas reached for the dipper in the bucket of cool water he'd pulled from the creek earlier. While there was a chill in the air, the sun was still bright, and something about that made him thirsty. Or maybe it was the fear that his face was on one of those posters inside the hotel lobby right this moment. Or the guilt at what he'd done that ate at him if he thought too much about it.

He pulled off his hat, reached for another ladle of water, and dumped this one over his head. Dropping the dipper back into the bucket, he rubbed at the cold liquid trickling its way through his hair and into his eyes. That did the trick. His mind sharpened just enough to remind him that he didn't necessarily know there was sketch of him in that sheath of paper. After all, wouldn't one of the front desk employees have recognized him and sent McFarland after him? Although it hadn't even been an hour yet . . .

A woman emerged from the kitchen door, interrupting his worried thoughts.

And not just any woman. She was the one who'd caught his eye more than once since Hartley's wedding.

Her arms were filled with a wooden crate of glassware, and she kicked the kitchen door shut with her foot. She set the crate down next to one of the fussy wrought iron chairs that someone had pulled from the nearby garden. Then she settled herself onto the equally fussy floral cushion and reached into the crate. She pulled out a piece of stemmed glassware and began rubbing at it with a cloth.

Thomas couldn't take his eyes off her, and she hadn't even noticed him.

Eventually he realized he must look a fool, standing there, covered in sawdust, water dripping down his shirt, and staring at this girl who looked as if she'd blown in on the breeze. He shook his head and clamped the worn brown hat back on it.

The shelving. He needed to get back to this project, or else McFarland would have no use for him.

Rather than waste the wood he'd already worked with, he decided to trim off the notches on each piece and try again. This one could be a smaller shelf to hang just inside the door for those items used most often. He began to saw into the wood, letting the misshapen notches he'd made earlier fall to the ground.

"Pardon me." A higher-pitched voice sounded over the grind of metal through wood. "Pardon me!" it said again as he yanked the saw through the last bit of wood.

He looked up, knowing exactly who he'd find in front of him.

And he wasn't wrong.

The petite blonde girl stood in front of him, one hand on her hip, the other one holding out a delicate glass. She wore the soft gray dress and white apron that all the Gilbert Girls wore under a black cloak, and a small, matching gray hat perched on her head.

"Good morning, miss," he said as he pulled off his hat and ran a hand over his wet hair. His words were smooth, but his heart leapt in a strange way to see her this close to him.

"Good morning," she said shortly. "Would you mind terribly if I asked you to relocate your . . . woodworking?"

She looked a bit ruffled, and something about that delighted him. But he schooled his face into an impassive expression. The last thing he wanted was for this beautiful woman to think he was laughing at her. "How come?"

The woman held out the glass. He looked at it, but all he saw was, well, a glass.

She shook it a little in her small hand. "You're getting sawdust in the stemware."

He stepped around the table and peered into the glass. One tiny piece of sawdust sat on the side of the glass. He reached in, pressed it against his finger, and lifted it out. "Fixed," he said, holding his finger out to the girl.

She stared at his hand as if he held a dead mouse in his palm. "You dirtied it! Now I have to wash the glass and let it dry before I can rub the spots off it." Her words were so carefully formed, almost as if she were speaking to the Queen of England and not a man born and raised in Texas by a barkeep father. He had only scant memories of his mother, but according to his father's tales, she would've gotten along well with this pretentious, fussbucket of a girl.

The way she kept looking so appalled at his hand made it impossible to keep the laughter in. It burst out like a winter gale. "I apologize for sullying your glassware. But to be truthful, no one is going to notice one tiny piece of sawdust in a glass."

She drew herself up to her fullest height, still nearly a foot shorter than Thomas. Wisps of wheat-colored hair floated around her face and her blue eyes shot fire at him. "The Gilbert Company does *not* serve its guests from glasses with even the tiniest speck of dust, sir. Now will you kindly move your table away from my work area?"

He couldn't keep the grin off his face. She was livid. That made him only want to poke at her more, almost to see if she'd drop her high-society facade. "No, ma'am. I don't believe I can. You see, I set up here first—at the request of the head chef—and here I intend to stay. You'd best find yourself a new place to scrub at your glassware or just get used to filling it with *all* of this sawdust."

The girl's face went bright red. "I—" She didn't finish, only clamped her mouth shut and spun on her heel back to her chair.

Thomas laughed to himself as she picked up her crate and marched away toward the garden. She was awfully pretty, he admitted to himself as he picked up a knife and the recut piece of wood. Beautiful, in fact.

But far too prim for his liking.

GET THE REST OF *Running From Forever* here: http://bit.ly/RunningForeverBook

Want to know when the next *Gilbert Girls* book is available to read? Sign up here: http://bit.ly/catsnewsletter

You can also join the fun on Facebook at: http://bit.ly/CatonFacebook and on my website http://bit.ly/CatCahillAuthor

About the Author, Cat Cahill

A sunset. Snow on the mountains. A roaring river in the spring. A man and a woman who can't fight the love that pulls them together. The danger and uncertainty of life in the Old West. This is what inspires me to write. I hope you find an escape in my books.

I live with my family, my hound dog, and a few cats in Kentucky. When I'm not writing, I'm losing myself in a good book, planning my next travel adventure, doing a puzzle, attempting to garden, or wrangling my kids.

Manufactured by Amazon.ca
Bolton, ON